# The Tree with a Golden Heart

Other books in this series

*A Surprisingly Fluffy Bird*

*The Magical Midwinter Star*

Jenny Chapman

# The Tree with a Golden Heart

AN SITHEAN PRESS

The Tales from the Adventures of Algy series
is supported by Algy's web site for children,
where young readers can learn about Algy's world,
add their own pictures and poems, ask questions,
look up words in Algy's online dictionary,
and discover many fluffy surprises.

adventuresofalgy.com

First edition 2015
Second edition 2017

Published by An Sithean Press, an imprint of MacAvon Media
Achnaha House, Kilchoan, Acharacle PH36 4LW Scotland (UK)

ISBN: 978-1-910637-08-1

Printed in the UK by W & G Baird

# Contents

## ≈ Chapter 1 ≈
## The Babbling Bog Fever

"Algy!" shrieked a tiny high-pitched voice. "Algy! Algy! Wake up, Algy! Wake up, Algy! Wake up!"

Algy rolled over slowly, lifted his wing off his head for a moment, peeped out blearily through a small heart-shaped gap in the dense curtain of green ivy that screened his nest, and turned back over again. "'S'too early," he mumbled. "Come back later."

"Algy, wake up!" squeaked the little voice again, and it had a shaky sort of tremble to it. "Algy, you must wake up! It's Plog! Please wake up, Algy. It's Plog!"

"Doesn't sound like Plog," murmured Algy, curling himself up and tucking his head back underneath his fluffy wing.

"Algy, you must wake up," insisted the tiny voice. "It's Plog! Plog's ill. He's taken the fever. They need you. Please wake up!"

"What?" mumbled Algy. "Plog's a squirrel? That's silly. G'back to sleep."

Suddenly Algy felt a sharp little nip on his toe. "Sorry Algy," squeaked the tiny voice. "But you've got to wake up. Please! Plog's awful sick."

Algy rolled onto his back and raised his head. "Plog?" he said. "You mean Plog is ill? Plog the frog?" Shaking his feathers, Algy eased himself up and leaned back drowsily against the mound of dry heather flowers and soft birch leaves which he used as a pillow. He rubbed his eyes and peered at his foot in the dim half-light; he could just make out the shape of a little mouse hopping up and down beside his toes. "Is that you, Wee Katie?" he said. "I can't quite see you. What's all the fuss about?"

"It's Katie's cousin, Wee Davie," squeaked the mouse. "Katie didna fancy climbing all the way up here. She's away down there, waiting." The mouse waved a tiny hand towards the entrance to Algy's nest. "Algy," squeaked Wee Davie, "you're needed in the bog. Plog's awful sick. He's taken the bog fever. Old Eachann sent

2

word to fetch you right away. Are you awake? Will you go right away?"

"What?" said Algy, alarmed. "Is it serious? I'll go at once. Are you going too? What's the bog fever? Is Plog all right? Where is he? Is he in the bog? Who's there to help him? Shall I fly, or go with you?"

"Fly!" squeaked Wee Davie. "Fly! Fly! Fly! Fly! Fly! Old Eachann says you're to go right away. You can ask him all your questions."

Rubbing his eyes again very quickly, to get the rest of the sleepiness out of them, Algy swivelled round and scrambled to his feet. Crying "Hold on tight!" he swept the horrified Wee Davie up under one wing, shoved the ivy curtain aside, swooped out of his cliff-side doorway, and plummeted down in front of the sheer cliff wall to the ground below.

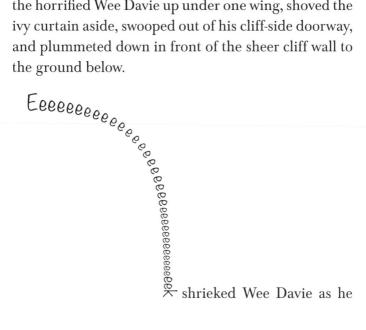

Eeeeeeeeeeeeeeeeeeeeeeeeeeeeeeeeeeeeek shrieked Wee Davie as he hurtled through the air, clutching frantically on to Algy's wing feathers with his tiny hands.

"Eeeeeeeeeeeeeeeeeeeeeeeeek," squealed Wee Katie as Algy dropped her flying cousin right on her tail with a bump.

"Oh, I'm sorry!" said Algy, who was in such a state of distress that he didn't really know what he was doing. "Are you all right, Wee Katie? Are you all right, Wee Davie? I'm terribly sorry."

"Aye, aye, I'm fine except for the tail," squeaked Wee Katie, massaging her sore tail gently with her furry nose. "But don't mind me. It's only a tail. Away to the bog!"

"Eeeeeeeeeeeeek," squeaked Wee Davie again. "I'll no' be doing that again in a hurry!" The little mouse darted away under a bush, to make sure that Algy couldn't reach him. "I'll be walking the rest of the way, thank you. You go on ahead now, and we'll be following in a wee while."

Algy tipped his head back and studied the sky for a moment. It was a dark, inky blue overhead, but above the crags in the distance a long, faint streak of light was steadily growing larger as it began to turn pink and gold. The full moon was just sinking down behind the ridge on the other side, and the surface of the sea was shimmering with a silvery-pink glow. Algy could see that some of the sea birds were already up and about, looking for their breakfast. It was very nearly daytime.

"All right, I'll see you there," said Algy, and jumping back into the air he flew off towards Plog's bog as swiftly as he could in the dim light, following the pale stretches of sand along the beaches. The grasses on the dunes sighed and waved in the morning breeze like spiky ghosts as he passed by, and the oystercatchers who were foraging on the tideline called out to him with their plaintive voices, "Queeeeeeek, quick, quick, quick, quick, quick, quick, quick! Queeeeeeek, quick, quick, quick, quick, quick, quick, quick, quick!"

"I'm going as fast as I can," cried Algy, as he swept over the last stretch of sand and low rocks which led to the headland. He was just about to cross the Blue Burn, when he heard someone else calling up to him from below.

"That cannot be you Algy, surely?" snuffled a familiar voice. "What would you be doing, rushing about at this time of the morning?"

Algy looked down, and saw that his friend Ruaridh the rabbit was sitting just outside the entrance to his home in the peat bank above the Blue Burn, carefully cleaning his whiskers. Algy descended rapidly, and landed beside Ruaridh. "Haven't you heard?" gasped Algy breathlessly. "It's Plog. He's very ill. The mice came to fetch me. They woke me up. I'm to go at once. There's no time to lose."

"And what might be ailing the Bard of the Bog?" sniffed Ruaridh.

"Something called the bog fever," said Algy. "Do you know what that is?"

Ruaridh shivered, and twitched his whiskers. "Is that so?" he snuffled quietly. "The bog fever! I'm sorry to hear that."

"Is it bad?" said Algy.

"It's no' very good, to be sure," sniffed Ruaridh. "But he'll maybe recover." Ruaridh paused, and twitched his whiskers thoughtfully. "Sometimes they do, and sometimes they don't," he snuffled quietly.

"Don't recover!" exclaimed Algy, more alarmed than ever. "You don't mean..."

"It's maybe not that bad," snuffled Ruaridh. "You'd best be going right away, though. I'll see you later."

"All right," said Algy, who was beginning to shake. "I'll get there as soon as I can."

"Who was it sent the mice to you?" sniffed Ruaridh.

"Old Eachann, I think," said Algy. "I was fast asleep when they came. It was Wee Katie's cousin Wee Davie who woke me, but I can't quite remember exactly what he said."

"Old Eachann will know what to do," snuffled Ruaridh. "Don't you fret yourself. Just fly away up there and give them a hand. I'll be up in a wee while, to see what I can do."

"Yes, please come soon," cried Algy, leaping hurriedly back into the air, and he turned away towards the bog.

Plog's home was not far from the Blue Burn, so in a few moments more Algy could see the water of the bog pools gleaming in the early morning light. As he approached, he recognized the unmistakable figure of Old Eachann, who was standing with his feet submerged in the shallow water, apparently giving orders to a small group of mice and birds who were gathered around him on the drier tussocks of long grass that grew out of the spongy bog. The stately old heron towered above the rest of the creatures, bending his long neck slowly this way and that as he spoke. Algy couldn't hear what he was saying, but the creatures were listening very attentively.

Flying closer, Algy began to descend over the large rocky outcrop that sheltered the bog from the ocean winds, and suddenly spotted Mr Voles, who seemed to be dashing about madly in all directions across the rock, frantically biting shiny green leaves off the low straggly bushes which grew in the crevices and around the base of the rock. Two or three mice were also scampering about behind Mr Voles, collecting up the leaves and carrying them away towards Old Eachann, leaping from tussock to tussock as they crossed the wetter areas of the bog.

Algy landed on the rock and tried to give Mr Voles a fluffy hug, but he couldn't catch his furry friend. "Not a moment to lose, not a moment to lose," gasped Mr Voles as he darted past Algy's foot.

"What are you doing?" asked Algy. "Why so many leaves?"

"So many leaves," echoed Mr Voles, nuzzling Algy quickly with his furry nose as he whizzed past him again. "So many leaves!"

"But what are they for? Do they help with the bog fever?" said Algy.

"Bog fever, bog fever," murmured Mr Voles unhappily, in a wobbly little voice. "Bog fever, bog fever, bog fever."

Algy stared towards the spot where Old Eachann was standing. Very little seemed to be happening, except for the frantic activity of Mr Voles and the leaping mice. As Algy watched them jumping from one tuft of grass to another, he realized that there were not just two or three mice carrying the leaves, but a whole relay team which stretched all the way from the rock to the bog pools. He was surprised to see that were carrying leaves both ways, backwards and forwards.

"Why are the mice carrying leaves both ways?" he called out to his furry friend, as Mr Voles shot past.

"Leaves both ways," puffed Mr Voles. "Fresh leaves out, stale leaves back; fresh leaves out, stale leaves back," and he rushed away.

Algy looked over towards Old Eachann, and saw that the heron had turned towards him.

"Ah, Algy," crackled the heron. "It is good that you have come." Lifting his long, spindly legs very carefully, one at a time, and sinking his feet down slowly and squelchily into the bog with every step, he moved towards Algy. "I am sorry to say that poor Plog has contracted the bog fever."

Old Eachann dipped his head towards a particularly large tussock of long grass, which rose out of the soggy ground right at the edge of the bog pools. "But Plog has always enjoyed your company," crackled the heron. "Your presence may comfort him."

"May comfort him," agreed Mr Voles, as he dashed across the rock past Algy's feet again, and then paused for a moment to bite off several more leaves.

"What is this bog fever?" Algy asked Old Eachann. "Is it really serious? Ruaridh said..." but then he tailed off shakily.

"It is known as the bog fever because it infects only the creatures who live in the bog," crackled Old Eachann. "It is not common, but from time to time it breaks out in the bog at this time of year, especially if the summer has been particularly wet. Most of the bog creatures have developed some resistance to it, so although they may catch the disease, it passes quickly and does them little harm. But occasionally it infects an unlucky creature who has no resistance, and then the full bog fever develops. It is rare indeed for this to happen, but when it does it becomes one of our most dreaded diseases. Poor Plog has been most unfortunate. I regret to say that he is not at all well."

"Not at all well," murmured Mr Voles glumly, as he scurried past them again. "Not at all well."

"I'll go and see him at once," said Algy, and jumping back into the air he flew straight across to the bog pools, passing low over the heads of the leaping mice. Flapping his wings as softly as he could, he cautiously approached the grassy tussock which hid Plog's sickbed. As he flew nearer, he heard a strange, hoarse, sing-song voice, which seemed to be chanting a nonsense rhyme.

*"Silly-illy froggly-woggly,*
*In the chilly soggly-boggly;*
*Ploggly-oggly-cloggly-goggly,*
*All a-foggly in his noggly."*

On and on the croaky chanting went, repeating the same rhyme over and over and over again in a peculiar voice that rose and fell with the rhythm of the words.

"Is that you, Plog?" said Algy, almost in a whisper, as he landed on the edge of Plog's tussock. But the voice just kept on chanting

*"Silly-illy froggly-woggly,*
*In the chilly soggly-boggly;*
*Ploggly-oggly-cloggly-goggly,*
*All a-foggly in his noggly."*

"Plog," said Algy, raising his voice slightly, "it's Algy. Your friend Algy. I've come to see you."

Plog paused in his chanting for a moment, but he didn't answer.

Old Eachann stalked forward, putting his feet down very gingerly as he made his way through the squelchy bog. Stretching his long neck out towards Algy, he crackled quietly, "I should have warned you. Plog is delirious, and you should not expect to get much sense out of him, even if he recognizes you. The bog fever infects the brain, and Plog does not know what he's croaking. Some folk call it the babbling bog fever, because those who fall ill with it always babble nonsense."

"Oh, I see," said Algy sadly. "Poor Plog!" He leaned carefully over the tops of the long grasses that screened Plog's bed, and peered into the centre of the tussock. There lay Plog, sprawled on his stomach on a pile of green leaves, with a white half-shell full of water beside his head. Plog's eyes looked bulgier than ever, and parts of his head seemed to be bulging in an odd way too, but the rest of his body looked strangely thin and scrawny, and his legs were sticking out at peculiar angles.

"Hello Plog," said Algy gently. "How are you feeling?"

For a moment there was no response, then Plog rolled his eyes very slowly and blinked.

"It's Algy," said Algy again. "I've come to keep you company."

Plog blinked again, and then he began to chant hesitantly, in that strange, sing-song croak,

*"Algy...*
*...walgy,*
*Good...*
*...old palgy,*
*Won't...*
*... you sing me...*
*... a song?"*

Algy was relieved to find that Plog knew who he was, but his poor friend was certainly not at all well, just as Old Eachann had said.

"I'm so very sorry that you are ill," said Algy. "I'm going to help look after you, until you feel better."

But Plog just repeated, a little more smoothly,

*"Algy-walgy,*
*Good old... palgy,*
*Won't... you sing me a song?"*

All of a sudden Algy heard a shrill squeak, and a tiny mouse jumped over to Plog's tussock from a neighbouring one, with its mouth full of fresh green leaves. It placed the leaves carefully around Plog, one at a time, picked up two or three brown leaves which were looking shrivelled and dry, then leaped away and vanished among the long grasses.

"Plog must be provided with a constant supply of fresh bog myrtle leaves," crackled Old Eachann. "The bog myrtle is the only remedy we have to fight the fever. He must have fresh bog myrtle leaves, and plenty of good, clean water to drink."

12

"Shall I refill his water?" Algy asked, reaching down towards the little shell by Plog's head.

"Take no water from the bog!" crackled the heron sharply. "It's the bog water that carries the fever. Plog must have only the fresh water that comes from the free-running burn. The hooded crows are bringing it."

Algy sniffed the air. There was a soothing, aromatic fragrance coming from the fresh leaves around Plog's bed; he could believe that they might help to banish the fever. "There's a large patch of those bog myrtle bushes near my nest," he said. "I didn't realize what they were before, but I noticed their lovely smell. I could fetch some more leaves from there."

"I'm afraid they would dry out too much on the way," crackled Old Eachann. "The leaves start to dry as soon as they are picked, and quickly lose their healing powers. They should be taken from the nearest supply, and changed frequently."

"There must be something I can do," said Algy sadly.

"I think you should remain beside Plog and keep him company," crackled the heron. "Someone should stay with him, and he may feel calmer if he knows that you are here. He recognized you, which is a good sign. You could sing to him sometimes, as he suggested, and talk to him when he is awake. It will cheer him up, and perhaps prevent his mind from wandering. Mr Voles and the mice can manage the bog myrtle leaves, and there is not much else that anyone can do. We must just watch and wait."

"Of course," said Algy, and leaning down close to the frog he whispered gently, "I'll be right here beside you, Plog, and I'll sing to you and tell you stories, and very soon you'll be well again, and then we'll make up lots of new rhymes together."

*"Algy-walgy,*
  *Good old palgy,"*

croaked Plog faintly, in his strange, sing-song voice, and then stopped. He seemed to have suddenly fallen asleep.

Algy looked up at Old Eachann, worried.

The heron tipped his head sideways and listened, then bent his long neck down low over Plog's bed and laid his ear lightly against the prostrate frog for a moment. Straightening up again, he nodded reassuringly at Algy. "Do not be too concerned," he crackled. "Plog will be drifting in and out of consciousness. That is the way of the fever. For most of the time it is better for Plog to sleep. The fever and the daylight will be hurting his head while he lies awake. When the crows bring more water you can splash a little on his head and on his toes. We must try to keep him cool while the fever burns, and a frog is inclined to suffer in his toes. If the day grows warm later on, you should fan him gently with your wings, and shade his eyes from the light."

"I'll do that," said Algy. "I'll do whatever I can."

Old Eachann nodded. "I must speak with some of the other creatures," he crackled. "I will return later. If you should need me before then, call loudly, or send a mouse to fetch me." He turned away and began to stalk back through the bog towards a group of birds and animals who had gathered at the base of the rock where Mr Voles was collecting leaves.

As Old Eachann approached the rock, Algy noticed that Ruaridh the rabbit was among the creatures crowding around the heron. Algy waved a wing at his friend, who waved a furry foot back at him, but Ruaridh did not cross the bog to speak to him.

Algy could not hear their conversation, but he could see that Old Eachann was talking earnestly to Ruaridh, gesturing at the higher rocky areas of the headland, and in a moment or two more the rabbit dashed away. As he hopped along the base of the big rock, and then up a steep slope in the direction of the Singing Place, his white tail bobbed up and down like a bouncing ball of fluff. Algy wondered where his friend could be going in such a hurry, and why. He couldn't see much sense in sending Ruaridh up to the Far View Rocks, especially as a bird would get there faster, so the next time a mouse hopped over to Plog's tussock with a supply of fresh bog myrtle leaves, Algy asked "Where's Ruaridh going?"

But the mouse just squeaked, "I dinna ken," and leaped away again.

## ≈≋ Chapter 2 ≋≈
### Algy-Walgy, Sing Me a Song?

The peat bog was hushed and quiet in the early autumn sunshine, and everything was calm and still. Occasionally, Algy could hear Old Eachann crackling quietly to some of the creatures who came to enquire about Plog, and sometimes he heard the mice squeaking as they arranged their relay service of fresh leaves, but most of the time there was almost no noise at all, except the buzzing of a late bee, or the flittering sound of a butterfly who had not yet found a home for the coming winter.

16

Checking that Plog had not woken up, Algy extracted his feet from the bog, where they had been sinking down into the strange, spongy cushion of some soggy plant, and carefully manoeuvred himself onto a small heather bush which was growing out of the edge of Plog's tussock. It was not exactly a comfy perch, but it provided a good view of his sick friend's bed.

Plog seemed to be very fast asleep now, so there was little that Algy could do for him. Tipping his head back as he wriggled into a slightly better position, Algy gazed moodily up at the clear blue sky, and tried to focus on composing a special song for Plog, but it was very difficult to concentrate with his friend lying unconscious in his bed. His mind kept wandering and worrying, and instead of a new song Algy found that he was beginning to chant poor Plog's nonsense rhyme inside his own head:

"Silly-illy froggly-woggly,
    In the chilly soggly-boggly;
    Ploggly-oggly-cloggly-goggly,
    All a-foggly in his noggly."

That would never do! Algy shook himself up, and tried again to work on his own song.

As he stared at the sky, Algy noticed two birds flying close together, approaching from the direction of the Blue Burn. They were silhouetted against the light, but as they flew nearer he could see that they were a pair of hooded crows. One seemed to be carrying a large, pitcher-shaped shell in its beak, and the other was flying a little way ahead, crying "Cawwwwwwww, cawwwwwwww, cawwwwwwwwwww. Cawwwwwwww, cawwwwwwww, cawwwwwwww, cawwwwwwwwwww," as though to warn everyone to keep out of their way.

Algy didn't know the crows very well. He met them occasionally, but they usually stayed further inland and kept to themselves. They were exceptionally clever and agile, but difficult to talk to, being birds of few words. Algy couldn't help feeling a little nervous in their company, although he admired their ingenuity.

"Cawwwwwwww, cawwwwwwww, cawwwwwwww, cawwwwwwwwwwwww," the first crow cried again, as it landed on another heather bush close to Algy. "Cwww, cwww, cwwwww," muttered the second crow, whose mouth was full of the large shell. It circled overhead, and then dropped down precisely on the edge of Plog's tussock. Balancing on one leg, the crow leaned over the grasses towards Plog's bed and lifted its other foot up to the shell in its beak. Very carefully, it tipped its head forwards, holding on to the edge of the shell with its toes, and poured a stream of clear water out of the jug shell, into Plog's drinking shell. Then it lifted the jug shell back into the air, turned it around in its beak, and gently sprinkled the last few drops of water over Plog's head and toes.

"Frog's asleep," it cawed to Algy. "How's he doing?"

"He was awake not very long ago," said Algy. "He spoke to me. That is, he babbled a rhyme."

18

"That's good," cawed the crow.

"Shall I help you fetch the water?" asked Algy. "I'd be happy to take a turn. It must be hard work."

"Nae bother," cawed the crow, and hopping sideways a few steps to the edge of Plog's tussock, it cocked its head on one side, winked twice at Algy, and then swept up into the air and away towards the burn, crying "Cawwwwwwww, cawwwwwwww, cawwwwwwwww" as it flew. The second crow quickly flew up to join it, and they sped away together crying "Cawwwwwwww, cawwwwwwww, cawwwwwwwwwwww," in turns.

Algy leaned over towards Plog's leafy bed. "Plog, are you awake?" he asked quietly, but there was no answer. Plog had not moved, and still seemed to be fast asleep.

"Poor old Plog," whispered Algy sadly. Reaching down, he crushed a couple of the leaves at the edge of Plog's bed, to release the healing vapours, and their lovely, aromatic fragrance filled the air once again, lifting his spirits a little. As the day was getting warm, Algy fanned Plog gently with his wings, and then settled down in his heather bush to watch and wait.

The sun climbed up to the top of the sky, and then started to slip back down again towards the sea. The mice hopped about with the bog myrtle leaves, sometimes pausing to exchange a few words with Algy before they carried on with their task. The hooded crows brought fresh shellfuls of water, cawing and winking at Algy each time they arrived. And, from time to time, Old Eachann stalked across the bog to

19

look at Plog, and then returned to his position by the rock, where he directed the mice and other creatures, and answered enquiries from the friends who came to ask after the sick frog.

But Ruaridh the rabbit did not return. Algy grew more and more curious about where he had gone, and as the day wore on he began to worry about his rabbit friend too. When Old Eachann came over to see Plog again, the sun was sinking low in the sky and there was still no sign of Ruaridh, so Algy asked him, "Where has Ruaridh gone to? I saw him leave this morning, and he hasn't come back. He has been away all day now. Is he all right?"

"Ruaridh has gone on an important mission, but there is no cause for concern," crackled the heron. "I have sent him to look for Brianag, the ancient lizard of Dùn Bàn. The search may take some time."

"The ancient lizard of Dùn Bàn?" said Algy, surprised. "Whoever is that?"

"Brianag is an exceedingly old lizard," crackled Old Eachann. "She has lived a life much longer than most of her kind, and far longer than the rest of us here. She has an unusual knowledge of certain things, and the special wisdom of her years. It is possible that she could help Plog, or provide us with advice. But Brianag is a recluse, and she is never easy to find. She lives alone and hates to be disturbed, especially when the days are getting shorter and the nights are growing colder. She will be making herself ready for her annual hibernation. Even when she is more active it can take many days to find her, but at this time of year it may be impossible."

"Do you really think she could help?" Algy asked eagerly.

"Perhaps," crackled the heron quietly. "Perhaps. That will depend on the course that the fever takes. But Ruaridh has not returned, and it may be that he will fail to find her. For now, we must simply continue to watch and wait."

And so Algy and his friends watched and waited, and waited and watched, and watched and waited again, day after worrying day, and night after weary night. Algy whiled away the time by composing his special song for Plog, and then sang it to him quietly while he slept, hoping that it would help to soothe and comfort his sick friend.

The first few times that Algy sang there was no indication that Plog could hear him, but Algy continued to sing nevertheless, and eventually Plog seemed to take some notice. He blinked slowly at Algy, then croaked in strange, hoarse, sing-song voice:

"*Algy-walgy,*
 *Good old palgy,*
 *Why don't you sing me a song?*"

"Hello Plog," said Algy. "I'm glad you've woken up. I have been singing you a song – a special song that I made up just for you. Would you like to hear it?"

Plog just croaked

*"Good old palgy,*
    *Why don't you sing me a song?"*

"I'll do that," said Algy. He sprinkled Plog's head with a little water from the white drinking shell, and crushed some of the bog myrtle leaves to release the vapours. Then he started to sing again, in a quiet voice.

"My friend is a poet, he's clever and funny,
    They call him the Bard of the Bog;
    He is witty and smart
    And knows verses by heart,
    And he goes by the short name of Plog.

He is praised for his wonderful way with a ditty,
    He makes up a rhyme at great speed;
    So if ever you're sad,
    Or are just feeling bad,
    Good old Plog is the friend that you need.

Plog croaks just in rhyme, and if you have time
    He will thrill you with poems all day;
    His rhymes will delight you,
    His stories excite you;
    Your blue mood will vanish away.

If I find that I'm not feeling quite as I ought to,
    Or things are not going so well,
    I just call on my chum,
    For whenever I'm glum,
    He will find a droll story to tell.

Now Plog is himself feeling under the weather,
And so I am singing this song,
To help to relieve a
Good friend with the fever,
And stop him being ill very long.

So cheer up my friend, you will soon feel better,
Your head will be free from the pain;
Then we'll laugh and we'll rhyme,
And have such a good time
That you'll never be poorly again."

*"Algy-walgy,"* croaked Plog hesitantly, blinking at Algy again. *"Algy-walgy, sing me a song?"*

"Of course," said Algy, and fanning Plog gently with his wings, he crooned his song again in a low, soft voice, as though it were a lullaby, until his friend went quietly back to sleep.

Together with Mr Voles, who always snuggled up beside him as soon as it got dark, Algy watched over Plog every night. As one night followed another, the moon waned steadily, until it was just a pale sliver in the sky, but still Ruaridh the rabbit did not return.

And then at last, early one morning, Ruaridh's familiar shape bounced into sight. Algy was so relieved that he shouted to his friend as soon as he saw him, "Ruaridh, are you all right? Where on earth have you been?" forgetting for a moment that he might alarm the sleeping Plog. But Plog did not wake up, and Ruaridh bobbed over, hopping from tussock to tussock, and gave Algy a big, reassuring rabbit hug.

"I'm still searching for Brianag," Ruaridh snuffled. "I've looked every place Old Eachann suggested, and some that he didn't, but she's no' there!"

"I hope you're taking care," said Algy. "I've been so dreadfully worried about you, away all this time."

"I'm not as daft as I look," sniffed Ruaridh. "Don't you fret, I'll be fine. How's he doing now?"

"He's not much better, but I don't think he's worse," said Algy.

"That's not so bad," snuffled Ruaridh. "That's not so bad at all. But I must see Old Eachann. He's no' going to be very pleased with me."

"It's not your fault," said Algy. "I'm sure you're doing the best you can."

"It's no' easy," sniffed the rabbit. "But I'm doing what I can, and that's all I can do," and giving Algy another hug he hopped away to speak to Old Eachann.

After that, Ruaridh returned to the bog quite frequently, but each time he had the same story to tell: he had looked here, there and everywhere, but had still not managed to find Brianag. Old Eachann seemed to think that the longer Plog lay sick with the fever, the more important it was to find the wise old lizard, so Ruaridh rarely stopped to chat with Algy, but dashed away again as soon as he had received new instructions from the heron.

Without anyone to talk to, the weary time of watching and waiting seemed even longer, and Algy began to feel that it would never end.

One lonely night, when the moon had entirely vanished from the sky, and Algy was staring into the darkness lit only by a faint glimmer of light from the stars and a hint of the approaching dawn, Ruaridh came bouncing across the bog and sat down on a tussock by his side.

"What's this?" snuffled the rabbit, peering closely at Algy in the dim light. "You're not looking so good, my friend. Do you not think you should get some rest? We're not needing a sick fluffy bird to look after too!"

Algy made an effort to wake up. "I do try to rest from time to time," he said wearily. "But I just can't seem to get to sleep if I go back to my nest. I lie awake worrying about Plog. I sleep here when I can, but I have to keep watch most of the time, and when I drop off I keep waking up to see what's happening."

"That's half a moon's passed now, since Plog fell sick," sniffed the rabbit thoughtfully, twitching his whiskers. "You fly away home and get a good rest. He'll still be here tomorrow."

"Do you really think so?" asked Algy. "How can you be sure?"

"There's nothing that's sure in this world," snuffled Ruaridh. "Except maybe that nothing is sure."

"Nothing is sure," murmured Mr Voles sleepily.

"But when the bog fever is going to take someone, it takes them sooner than this," Ruaridh continued.

"You mean Plog is going to get better?" cried Algy excitedly.

"Get better, get better, get better!" echoed Mr Voles.

"If Plog has held on this long, he'll no' be leaving us now," sniffed the rabbit.

"But if you think Plog will get better, why are you still searching for Brianag?" asked Algy. "I don't understand."

"Folk that manage to come out of the fever are no' themselves any more," Ruaridh snuffled quietly. "Old Eachann says Brianag knows something that will help."

"But you can't find her," said Algy. "You've looked everywhere, and still you haven't found her."

"I'll not be giving up just yet a while," sniffed Ruaridh.

"Why isn't Roni the raven helping?" asked Algy. "I keep wondering why she isn't here, or out looking for Brianag with you."

"Her business is up at the Far View Rocks," snuffled Ruaridh. "She'd be here if she was needed, but there's nothing she can do that other folk can't do as well. I've asked her about Brianag, and she has asked around. They all say the old lizard has not been seen for a wee while now. It's no' easy!"

"It's no' easy," agreed Mr Voles, as he set off towards the rocky outcrop where the bog myrtle grew.

Old Eachann made his way towards them, lifting his long, spindly legs high in the air as he stalked carefully through the wetter parts of the squelching bog.

"Ruaridh is right," he crackled as he approached. "It is time for you to rest now, Algy, or you may fall ill yourself. Go home and sleep peacefully. I will watch Plog myself this morning. You need not be concerned."

"You'll send for me if anything happens," Algy said. "Promise?"

"I will send a mouse running if we need you," crackled Old Eachann, "but I doubt that it will be necessary."

"All right," said Algy reluctantly. "If you're sure."

"That's right," Ruaridh snuffled. "You have a good, long sleep. Nothing will happen just now. And I'll be away back up to the rocks, on a wild lizard chase..."

"Do not give up the search," Old Eachann crackled to Ruaridh. "I am sure that you will find Brianag yet."

Algy yawned, and gave Ruaridh a big fluffy hug. "I hope you find her this time," he said drowsily.

"Away you go," snuffled Ruaridh, hugging his friend back. "I'll be seeing you." He bobbed across the bog from tussock to tussock, and then vanished out of sight.

"Get better," Algy whispered to the sleeping Plog, leaning down over his bed. "I'm going home to sleep, but I'll come back and see you again very soon."

Algy fluttered up into the air and started to head back towards his little home in the cliff face at the other end of the bay. He had not been paying much attention to the weather, but as he flew along he noticed that he seemed to be getting wet. Looking around, he saw that the mist was rolling down the hillsides, covering everything with a dripping grey blanket. Although it was still early morning, the sky was getting darker instead of lighter, and by the time Algy reached his nest he could see no further than the bushes which grew at the foot of the cliff. Pushing his way through the dripping ivy curtain that hung across his doorway, he crawled inside and curled up on his soft bed of dry heather flowers and silver birch leaves.

Whenever Algy had difficulty getting to sleep, he listened to the lullaby of the sea on the little beach nearby. Sometimes he could hear the waves pounding on the shore with a terrific roaring sound, and sometimes he could only hear a quiet whispering of gentle wavelets on the smooth sand at low tide. In wilder weather, the noise of the breakers crashing on the rocks beside the cliff drowned out the sounds of the beach entirely. But this time the drip, drip, dripping of the wet ivy and other plants around the entrance to his home merged softly and soothingly with the sound of the waves, which were rolling onto the sand with long, slow sighs in the dense mist

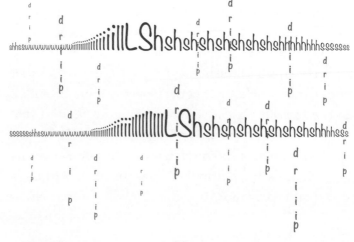

The waves rolled on as the tide washed in and out on the beach below, and the mist kept drip, drip, dripping, but Algy just slept and slept and slept and slept and slept.

Suddenly, a loud squeaking noise interrupted the other sounds. Algy sat up with a start and opened his eyes, but there was absolutely nothing to see. Everything was pitch black.

"Hello," he called. "Is somebody there?"

The squeaky little voice of a mouse answered from somewhere near the ivy curtain, "Algy, are you awake?"

"Of course I'm awake," Algy said anxiously. "I'm talking to you, aren't I? What's happened? Is something wrong? Is Plog all right?"

"It's Wee Katie," squeaked the voice. "I made it up here this time! I've good news and bad. The fever is away, and Plog is awake, but he's no' himself at all. And Ruaridh has found old Brianag at last."

"What do you mean, Plog's not himself at all?" said Algy, straining to see the little mouse by his doorway.

"It was Wee Davie that ran to tell me," squeaked Wee Katie. "He says Plog woke up just as it was getting dark, and he called right out, but what he said didna make any sense. A couple of my daft wee cousins went running right away, to fetch Old Eachann, and the heron came flying and checked him over from head to toe. Seems that the fever is away, all right. But Plog's no' himself any more."

"What's happened to him?" asked Algy.

"Wee Davie says that the Bard has no' got the rhymes any more, and he's awful fuddled in the head," squeaked the little mouse. "He's like a different creature altogether."

"I'll go over there at once," said Algy, looking uneasily at the blackness surrounding him.

"You're not to go just now," squeaked Wee Katie. "Old Eachann says you're not to trouble yourself tonight, and it's too black a night, to be sure. He just wanted to send word that the fever's away. You're to go at first light."

"Are you sure?" said Algy.

"Aye," squeaked Wee Katie. "And there'll be a wee meeting in the morning too, on account of old Brianag."

"I can't believe Ruaridh managed to find her at last," said Algy. "That's amazing! Where was she?"

"I'm no' very sure," squeaked Wee Katie. "You go back to sleep now, and I'll be away home. It's no' a fit night for blethering."

"Are you quite sure I shouldn't go over there tonight," Algy asked again.

"Aye. Did I not tell you? Old Eachann says you're not to come before morning. You get a good night's sleep now. Sweet dreams to you!"

"You too," said Algy, but there was no further reply; Wee Katie must have scurried away into the night.

Algy turned over and tried to go back to sleep, but having slept all through the day he did not find it so easy to drop off again, and for a long time he lay awake in his bed, tossing and turning in the darkness. In the depths of the night, the muffled noises of the sea and the drip, drip, dripping of the mist on the plants outside his door sounded surprisingly loud. Gradually, the sounds began to fill his whole mind, and then, at last, he drifted slowly off to sleep.

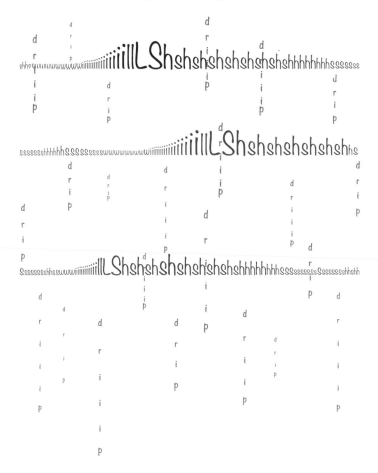

## ~~~ Chapter 3 ~~~
## The Ancient Lizard of Dùn Bàn

Algy woke up many times during that long, dark night, worrying about Plog, and afraid that he would miss the dawn. But every night must come to an end, and eventually he saw a tiny glimmer of grey light through the heart-shaped gap in his ivy curtain.

Massaging all his aches from the days and nights spent perching in the heather bush beside Plog's bed, Algy stuck his head out into the damp air and looked around. The mist had not lifted at all, and the world looked blurrily soft and grey in the half-light of dawn. Algy rubbed his eyes, shook himself thoroughly, and flew out of his doorway and up through the mist to the tiny burn that trickled down the hillside above his nest.

This was Algy's favourite place to bathe, as the stream flowed gently through many small, shallow pools surrounded by flat areas of rock before tumbling rapidly down the hillside to the sea. It was an ideal washing place for a fluffy bird, and before Plog's illness he had bathed there every morning.

Splashing himself quickly with the cool, fresh water, Algy began to feel a little better. There was no point trying to get dry, as the mist would soon make him wet again, so he just fluffed up his feathers as well as he could, flew back down the hillside, grabbed a large beakful of blackberries from the brambles beneath his nest, and set off along the beaches once more.

Each time he had flown this way since Plog fell ill, the weather had been dry and clear and Algy had been able to see all the islands in the bay, and far out to sea. But this time he couldn't even see the headland: the sand was grey and hazy beneath him, the ocean faded away into the dense cloud, and even the nearest islands were hidden in the mist. The dunes were looking more ghostly than ever, and the muffled cries of the invisible oystercatchers searching for their breakfast sounded quite eerie. The day had a strange sort of feeling to it, and Algy wondered what it would bring.

As he passed over the Blue Burn, Algy glanced down to see whether Ruaridh might be sitting outside his front door, but the peat bank was deserted and dark.

Algy assumed that his friend must have gone up to see Plog already, but when he arrived at the bog he could see no sign of Ruaridh there either. The wet mist drifted softly across the surface of the bog pools, covering every blade of grass with droplets of water and concealing the high rocky outcrops which surrounded Plog's home. Everything looked vague and unreal, as though it might fade away at any moment. The figure of Old Eachann was unmistakable, though, even in the mist; he was standing beside Plog's tussock, apparently talking to Plog. Flying over there quickly, Algy landed on his usual heather bush, which was now bent and battered from his perching on it for so long, and looked down into Plog's bed.

Plog was still lying on his stomach, but his eyes were wide open, and he spoke as soon as he saw Algy.

*"A bird of a feather.*
*Is it?*
*Often,"*

he croaked.

Algy was taken aback. He was not sure whether his friend had recognized him or not, but he certainly didn't sound quite right.

"I'm so very glad you're feeling better," Algy said. "We've been dreadfully worried about you."

*"Dreaming all day,*
*A fish.*
*Faint in the sky,"*

croaked Plog.

34

"A fish in the sky?" said Algy.

*"Down in the deep dark dense dank dreary drowsy*
                        *droopy-down dippy-in-the-depths,*
  *Dismal bog reeds.*
  *Murky all in clouds.*
  *Fins and tadpoles and something that swims..."*

croaked Plog, and he paused, blinking rapidly.

"Algy," crackled Old Eachann. "I would like to speak to you. Will you fly over to the rock and wait for me while I listen to Plog's breathing. I will join you in a moment." The old heron bent his long neck down over Plog's bed, and laid his ear against the frog's back.

*"Tickly, tickly, prickly-tickly,*
  *Feathers all like flies;*
  *Buzz, buzz, buzz away.*
  *Not!"*

croaked Plog, trying to wriggle away.

"I'll be back very soon," Algy said to Plog, and he flew slowly over to the edge of the large rocky outcrop where Mr Voles had gathered so many bog myrtle leaves. He was enormously relieved that Plog's fever had gone, but there was no doubt that his sick friend was "no' himself at all", as Wee Katie had said.

Old Eachann stalked across the bog, and stood in front of Algy. "The fever has definitely gone," the heron crackled quietly, "and Plog is now out of danger. But he is still by no means well, as you have seen. I am sure that his body will recover slowly as he begins to eat again, but his mind is badly damaged, I'm afraid. I was concerned that this would happen if he succeeded in fighting off the fever. It is said that there are few who survive the bog fever and live to tell a tale that makes sense."

"But won't his mind get better too?" Algy asked softly, not wanting Plog to be upset by what he said, now that his friend was awake and could be listening. "He has only just come out of the fever. Surely he will recover in time. He has been so ill, it must take quite a while to recover."

"Plog should certainly regain his strength in time," crackled Old Eachann, "but his mind may not recover, unless we can find him the proper medicine. This is not the first case of its kind. I'm afraid that the mind is sometimes permanently altered by the bog fever."

"That's terrible!" exclaimed Algy. "We must get him the medicine. What kind of medicine is it? Where can we find it?"

"This is why I have been so anxious to find Brianag," crackled the heron. "If Plog had not survived the fever, we would have had no need of her assistance. But I had hopes that Plog would recover, and I knew we would need her help once the fever had gone. There is no one else here now who knows the old medicine, and where to look for it. It is very fortunate that Ruaridh has managed to find her at last. Very fortunate indeed."

"Is she going to help us?" asked Algy. "I haven't seen Ruaridh yet, so I don't know what happened."

"Brianag had left her summer home, in preparation for the coming winter, but Ruaridh managed to find her eventually. She has agreed to attend a short meeting at the Singing Place today, when the sun is highest in the sky. As there will evidently be no sun, we must gather early and await her arrival. I understand that Ruaridh did not find it easy to persuade her to come. She was on the point of retiring for the cold, dark season, and was greatly annoyed at being disturbed. This weather will make matters worse, as she does not normally venture out in the cold or the mist. So I have sent Ruaridh to escort her to the meeting. I hope that he conducts himself well, as there is little we can do if Brianag will not help us. No one else has the knowledge any longer."

"Should we go straight up to the Singing Place now?" asked Algy. "It wouldn't do if she arrived when no one was there."

"No, indeed!" crackled the heron. "I think we should make our way up there now, as you suggest. I will ask two of the mice to stay with Plog, just in case things do not go well with him. I do not think that will happen, but the mice can come running, if it should prove necessary."

"I'll just have a word with him," said Algy, "and then I'll fly straight up there." Fluttering back over to Plog's bed, Algy perched on the heather bush and looked down at his friend.

"I have to go up to the Singing Place," he said, "but I'll come back and see you as soon as it's over."

*"That far old place,*
  *Singing rock, songs all drifting in the wind,*
  *Crashing sea,"*

croaked Plog hesitantly.

"Ummm, yes, that's right," said Algy reassuringly, not wanting to confuse his friend further. He patted Plog lightly with the tips of his wing feathers and jumped back into the misty air. "See you soon," he called.

Plog looked up at him and croaked

*"Soon*
  *Is not so much now,*
  *Or is it then, or sometime I forget?"*

"You get better now! I'll be back very soon," Algy called again, and then turned and headed for the Singing Place by the Far View Rocks.

On a fine day it was possible to see many islands from the Singing Place, with a view far out across the ocean, but as Algy came in to land on the large area of rough grass which surrounded the terraced rock, the mist was so thick that he could not even see the sea, although he could hear the familiar pounding of the waves on the jagged rocks far below.

Roni the raven, the Keeper of the Rocks, was standing on the highest point at the Singing Place, her black shape silhouetted against the pale mist. Various creatures were gathered on the rocky terraces below her, talking quietly to each other. Algy spotted Ruaridh chatting to Mr Voles on the upper level, and flew over to join them, giving each of them a big fluffy hug. Then a few moments later Old Eachann arrived, his huge wings flapping very slowly as he glided in to land. He stalked over towards Roni, and stopped a few paces away from her. "Has Brianag arrived?" he crackled.

Roni coughed and cleared her throat. "Quiet, please," she cried, in her loud rasping voice. "Quiet! The meeting will now commence." All the assembled creatures fell silent, except a couple of young mice who started to giggle. Roni glared at them, and continued.

"You all know why we are here," she rasped loudly. "Brianag, the venerable lizard of Dùn Bàn, has very kindly agreed to join us today to advise us in the matter of Plog's sickness. She has come here at great inconvenience to herself. Everyone will please remain silent while Brianag speaks."

Algy peered at Roni and the rock around her, but he could see no sign of any lizard. "She's there in front of you, there on the rock," snuffled Ruaridh quietly. "Look again!"

Algy looked again, and realized that what he had thought was a pattern of the tiny plants which sprawled out of the rock crevices was in fact a small lizard. She had stretched herself out across the vertical face of the highest rocky step at the Singing Place, and was clinging on to the rock, absolutely motionless.

Suddenly, Brianag lifted her head away from the rock and began to speak, slowly and very quietly, in a hushed, creaky, breathy sort of way. Her voice was scarcely more than a whisper, and if Algy had not known that she was speaking he would have mistaken the sound for the murmur of the wind through the dripping grasses all around them.

"One cure," Brianag breathed slowly. "One cure only, for the sickness of the mind that is the curse of the bog fever." She paused.

There was not a sound except the muffled roar of the sea on the rocks below, and the faint dripping and trickling of the land soaked in drenching mist.

"Crottle porridge," breathed the ancient lizard.

"Crottle porridge!" exclaimed Mr Voles in surprise.

"Crottle porridge," breathed the ancient lizard again. "The ancient mixture of the healing crottles from the old oak wood. Only that will cure your friend."

"What's a crottle?" Algy whispered to Ruaridh.

"Lichens," Ruaridh whispered back. "She means lichens. But there are so many different kinds. Far too many to try them all!"

"Hush," rasped Roni sharply. "There will be no disturbance."

The two young mice giggled again, and Ruaridh the rabbit hopped over to them and quickly placed a furry foot over each of their mouths.

"Please excuse the wee ones, Brianag," rasped Roni. "They are very young. Your advice is of the greatest importance to us."

"Use not the common crottle of the rocks," breathed the ancient lizard. "That has no power, except for colouring." She paused again with her mouth open, as though she was trying to catch more breath from the moist air, and then continued. "You must find the three healing crottles of the bark."

Brianag stopped, and this time she did not go on. There were a few moments of silence, and the young mice giggled quietly, muted by Ruairidh's furry paws.

Old Eachann bowed his head respectfully to the old lizard. "We thank you," he crackled. "And if we are able to find the healing crottles, how are we to use them?"

"In equal measures," Brianag sighed slowly and softly, like the wind approaching from the mountains across the wet heath. "In equal measures.

If you would make a crottle porridge,
You must have the ancient knowledge:
Three old lichens from the bark,
Gathered when the night is dark.
In equal measures, one by one,
Mashed in water till they're done;
Add two leaves of meadowsweet,
Then pound with stick or tread with feet.
Sup at morning, noon and night:
One sip at a time is right,
Until the mind is whole once more
Just as it was in times before."

Brianag breathed the old verse rhythmically, as though it were the faint, regular creaking of dry twigs in an autumn breeze.

Algy took a deep breath. He was somewhat overawed by the strange, ancient lizard, but he was absolutely determined to do whatever was necessary to help his friend get well. So, stepping forward, he spoke out, although he knew that it was not really proper for him to do so.

"Thank you so much," he said, speaking towards the rock face. "But could you please tell us where to find these crottles to make the porridge?"

The young mice giggled again, despite being silenced by Ruaridh's furry paws. Ruaridh swept them up with his front legs and bobbed away with them quickly into the rough grass that surrounded the Singing Place.

Roni stared at Algy, but she did not speak. The ancient lizard sighed "Whaaaaaaaaat?" and very slowly twisted her head round to look in Algy's direction.

"What is this?" she breathed "You are not of this place. What can this be to you?"

Algy was embarrassed, and suddenly felt like an awkward stranger again.

"I arrived here several moons ago," he said. "Before the spiky grasses of the dunes turned green. I travelled far across the sea on a raft, and was washed up on the beach. But this is my home now, and Plog is my friend. We make rhymes and songs together. That is, we used to... I want so much to help him get well again."

"Soooooooooooo..." breathed the ancient lizard in a whisper. "Soooooooooooo... Then perhaps this task will fall to you."

"Please tell me what I must do," said Algy shyly. "Where can I find these crottles?"

"You must seek the Tree with a Golden Heart," breathed the lizard in the faintest creaky voice, which murmured around the rocky platforms of the Singing Place like the sighing of the wind in the pine trees on a cold winter's night.

Several creatures gasped, including Ruaridh, who had returned quietly to his place by Algy's side.

"The Tree with a Golden Heart!" echoed Mr Voles nervously.

"At the time of the gloaming, on the first night that the new moon sinks down towards the hill, you must enter the Tree with the Golden Heart in the ancient woodland by the loch," sighed Brianag softly, and she paused to take another deep breath. "Lay yourself down to sleep in the heart of the tree. If your own heart is good and true, a faithful guide will come to you and help you find that which you seek."

"That which you seek," whispered Mr Voles.

Brianag's voice drifted slowly away across the rock like the gentle breeze around them that was muffled by the mist, and for a few moments nobody spoke.

"Is there no other way?" rasped Roni softly.

"No other way," Brianag sighed slowly. "No other way, unless you have the old knowledge for yourself.

But beware," she breathed. "Beware if your heart is not true, for there is also danger there."

"The dangers of the Tree with a Golden Heart are known to us," crackled Old Eachann.

"Brianag, we thank you with all our hearts for your wisdom and advice, and for coming here to join us today," rasped Roni. "We will do our best to find the crottles and heal our friend."

"Then I will retire," breathed the ancient lizard softly, like the whisper of a gently falling leaf when the summer ends. "There is no more to say. I wish you well." And as Algy gazed at the place on the rock face where the lizard was clinging, she seemed to vanish. One moment she was there, and the next she was not. He could hardly believe his eyes, but he supposed that she must just be able to move surprisingly fast.

Roni turned to the assembled creatures, who were looking sadly wet and bedraggled in the dripping mist.

"For those who do not know, Old Eachann will now explain the dangers of this undertaking, so that no one sets off without realizing what's involved."

Clearing his throat, Old Eachann started to address the crowd on the rocky platforms. "Apart from the usual risks of a journey away from home, which we all understand, and the challenge of finding the tree, it is said that the Tree with a Golden Heart holds three dangers for those who enter it but should have stayed away," he crackled.

The heron looked slowly from side to side at all the creatures present, and then continued. "Those who presume to seek guidance in the Tree with a Golden Heart with intentions that are mean or selfish may never return. The creatures of the night lie in wait for such folk..." He paused again.

"Those who are well intentioned, but foolish and easily distracted, may be led astray by a false guide and become lost in the depths of the wood without achieving their goal. And those whose hearts are not entirely strong and true may lose that which they sought, after they have found it."

"Does anyone know where this tree is?" asked Algy.

There was a sound of scuffling and muttering on one of the lower terraces of the Singing Place, and suddenly a young bunny rabbit, still fluffy behind the ears, hopped up beside Ruaridh. She turned to face the assembly, wrinkled her little nose, and began to recite rhythmically, in a small, snuffly voice:

"It's said that the Tree with a Golden Heart
  In the ancient oak wood stands apart,
  Near the point where the forest meets the shore
  And overhead the eagles soar;
  The hillside there climbs steep and high
  To barren summits in the sky,
  But the brae is clothed in oak and birch,
  And at its foot is the place to search,
  For the entrance to the wood is found
  Where silver loch meets rocky ground
  Near seven skerries, bleak and black.
  The deer have made a muddy track:

Ascend this path until you hear
The sound of water running near;
The trickling of the hidden burn
Is loudest at the point to turn.
Then, looking back at what you passed
You'll see the cloven tree at last;
With strange but warm unearthly light
Its heart glows golden in the night.
In the ancient wood it stands apart:
The eldritch Tree with a Golden Heart."

Ruaridh patted his young relative on the back. "That's fine, Flòraidh," he snuffled. "That's fine."

Turning to Algy, Ruaridh sniffed, "All the young folk learn the rhyme, and many more besides. But I don't know that anyone has ever seen the tree."

Roni coughed loudly and cleared her throat. "I have heard tell of creatures who have seen the tree, although I haven't met any myself, but I've not heard of anyone who has entered its heart in recent times."

Old Eachann spoke again. "There is no doubt that any attempt to find the crottles will involve a risky and perilous mission. This should not be undertaken lightly," he crackled, looking at Algy. "Not even by one who is ready and willing to go. It is not only difficult and dangerous, but also likely to fail."

"But the next new moon is almost here," said Algy anxiously. "Brianag said the tree must be found on the night we first see the new moon. And Plog can't wait another moon, he might be much worse by then."

"That is true," crackled the old heron. "And if anyone were to go, it must therefore be a bird. No animal could travel to that place in time for the coming new moon, and no creature of the sea could enter the woodland or the tree without enormous difficulty."

"It's a terrible risk," rasped Roni, looking at Old Eachann with a shining black eye. "It doesn't sound wise to me. We might lose one friend in the attempt to heal another."

"Indeed," crackled Old Eachann slowly. "Much as I wish to return Plog to full health, I fear it is ill advised."

"How far do you think it is?" asked Algy. "Do you know the place in the rhyme?"

"The journey to the seven skerries is said to be less than a morning's flight," rasped Roni. "But finding the tree when you get there is another matter entirely."

"Another matter entirely," murmured Mr Voles.

"Many have searched, for good reasons or for bad, but few if any have found the tree," Roni continued. "The rhyme makes it sound much easier than it is."

"I think perhaps we should meet again," crackled Old Eachann. "Let us all take a short time to consider what we have heard, and meet again at first light tomorrow. That should allow sufficient time to search for the tree, if indeed it can be found at all."

"I agree," rasped Roni. "We will meet here again tomorrow, at first light."

"Tomorrow, at first light," echoed Mr Voles.

## ‿❦ Chapter 4 ❦‿
### Silvie the Seal

The assembled creatures slowly left the Singing Place, some alone, and some in the company of their friends. The mist had not lifted at all during the meeting, and everyone was feeling thoroughly bedraggled and downcast. As Algy prepared to fly away he whispered in Ruaridh's ear, "I want to talk to you. Can I meet you outside your front door?"

"Do you mean now?" sniffed Ruaridh, twitching some of the water off his dripping whiskers.

"As soon as you get there," Algy said softly. "I'll fly on ahead. I want to stop and see Plog on my way."

"Right," snuffled Ruaridh. "I'll be seeing you," and he bobbed off into the mist, his white tail sprinkling droplets of water in every direction as he bounced across the rough grass.

Algy gave Mr Voles a large but very damp fluffy hug. "Be sure to look after Plog carefully when I'm not there," he said.

"Not there?" muttered Mr Voles. "Not there?"

"Well, I can't be there all the time, can I?" said Algy reassuringly. "So at the times when I'm not there, please take good care of Plog." He hugged Mr Voles again, and jumped into the air.

"Where are you going?" cried Mr Voles anxiously.

"Just to the bog," Algy called back. "Just to the bog. See you soon."

"See you soon," echoed Mr Voles uncertainly, and he watched unhappily as Algy flew away across the headland towards Plog's bog.

Even in the mist it did not take Algy long to reach Plog's bedside. Shaking the water off his feathers as he landed, he perched on the battered heather bush.

"How are you feeling now?" he asked his friend.

*"Dribbly drippy dip drip, all listening in the grass,*
  *Wet, wet, wet, wet.*
  *Clouds falling in,"*

croaked Plog.

"Yes indeed," said Algy, glad that his friend seemed to be reasonably alert, if not exactly in his right mind.

He bent his head down low over Plog's bed and spoke very quietly.

"Plog," he whispered, "I may be away for a day or two, but it won't be for long. I'll be back very soon, I promise. I'm going to try to find you some medicine."

Plog croaked,

*"Friendly, friendly,*
  *Fluffy, is it? Featherdown,*
  *So floaty bird, drifty far away.*
  *But moon is not quite yet*
  *All pale and shiny thin."*

Algy wondered whether there was any way that Plog could know what Brianag had said at the Singing Place. It seemed unlikely, but perhaps someone else had got there first and talked about the meeting.

"Don't you worry about me," said Algy softly. "I'll be all right. When you see that shiny thin moon, I'll be back. And the others will take good care of you while I'm gone. It won't be long at all."

*"Flap, flap,*
  *Not swimmy legs:*
  *All lost in the dark. Not, not, not!"*

"It's all right," whispered Algy again. "Don't worry." He glanced across the bog and saw that Old Eachann was gliding in to land, his huge wings flapping slowly like enormous leaves in the wind. "I have to go now," he whispered quickly to Plog, giving him a very gentle

50

fluffy hug. "You just get better, and I'll be back soon." Pretending that he had not seen Old Eachann, Algy took off quickly, without looking back, and flew away in the opposite direction, towards the Blue Burn.

As he dropped down through the mist to land beside Ruaridh's home in the peat bank, he could see that his friend was waiting for him there.

"You travelled fast!" said Algy. "I thought I would get here before you."

"I took a wee short cut," snuffled Ruaridh, twitching his nose. "I didn't want you flying off without saying goodbye."

"Oh! So you've guessed," exclaimed Algy.

"It was no' very difficult," sniffed the rabbit. "But I don't think you should go. I've not travelled far myself, as I may have mentioned, but I've heard folk's tales from time to time. And you've not even flown beyond the crags before. We could send someone else; someone who knew their way about, maybe. The hooded crows might do it. They're up for anything."

"Of course I'm going to go," said Algy. "You know that I must. This isn't a job for the crows, or for anyone else. They've all been very kind and helpful, but they don't care about Plog in the same way that I do. If what Brianag told us is true, I think only a special friend has a chance of finding that medicine."

"Maybe so," snuffled Ruaridh reluctantly. "Maybe so. But I don't like it."

"I don't like it much either," said Algy, "but I'm going to do it all the same. I'll set off at dawn, and I want you to tell them about it after I've gone, when you go to the meeting tomorrow morning. I can't tell them myself or they'll make such a fuss. I'm sure they will try to stop me. So I'll just slip away quietly, and that will be that."

"Well, I suppose if you must, you must," snuffled Ruaridh. "But you'll need to take care. And you'll be needing to know a wee bit more about it, I think. Here," he sniffed, turning his head towards the hole in the peat bank that was the entrance to his home. "Come on out here, young Flòraidh, and meet Algy."

The young bunny rabbit who had recited the rhyme at the Singing Place peeked shyly out of Ruaridh's front door.

"This is my wee niece Flòraidh," snuffled Ruaridh. "She's my niece on my father's sister's husband's sister-in-law's brother's side. Flòraidh's a fine one for the rhymes, and she knows another that will come in handy."

"Does she?" said Algy. "That's wonderful."

"She's a wee bit timid," sniffed Ruaridh, bouncing over to his doorway. He reached behind Flòraidh and pushed her forward, so that she hopped out into the open in front of Algy.

"Hello, Flòraidh," said Algy kindly. "I'm very pleased to meet you."

The young bunny rabbit twitched her little whiskers and wrinkled her furry nose.

"Could you please repeat the rhyme you recited at the meeting, to start with?" Algy asked the little bunny. "I need to memorize that one, I think."

"It's the other one you'll be needing the most," sniffed Ruaridh, "or you'll not find the tree at all."

"That's fine," said Algy. "I'll try to learn them both by heart if they're going to help me."

Flòraidh hopped forward a couple of steps, and settled back on her fluffy little tail. In her quiet, snuffly voice she carefully recited "The Tree with a Golden Heart" again, just as she had done at the meeting, and Algy repeated it after her.

At first he made some mistakes, but Ruaridh and his niece soon corrected them, and it wasn't long before Algy was word perfect. He was so used to making up songs and rhymes himself that he had no difficulty memorizing verses, and he started to hum a tune to make it even easier to remember.

"Now for the other one," said Algy. "Is that about the tree as well?"

"That it is!" sniffed Ruaridh. "On you go, young Flòraidh."

The little bunny rabbit rubbed her ears with her small furry paws, twitched her short whiskers, and wrinkled her nose again. Then she began to recite a new rhyme.

"Do you seek that hidden tree
Whose golden heart so few may see?
Is your motive fine and good?
Then climb the track into the wood.
In the gloaming, not before,
Enter through the heather door,
Then, as the crescent moon sinks low,
Close your eyes in its pale glow;
Prepare yourself for slumber deep,
Repeat these lines until you sleep:
'Golden heart of the ancient tree,
Send a trusty guide to me.'
And when you see the shining light,
Be not startled, take no fright.
State your purpose, clear and true,
And then a guide will come to you.
If at first you go astray,
A false guide may have led the way;
But do not falter, try once more:
Go back inside that golden door.
For ancient stories long have told
That those whose hearts are also gold
Will find a faithful guide, who'll lead
The way to what they truly need.
But if your heart is false or black,
Beware, for danger's at your back!
If you tell a lie in that golden light,
You'll surely perish in the night."

"Gracious!" said Algy, but he proceeded to memorize the rhyme in the same way as the first one.

"That's fine, young Flòraidh," snuffled Ruaridh. "Now you hop along in and get your lunch."

The little bunny rabbit bobbed shyly at Algy, then hopped back quickly to Ruaridh's front door.

"Thank you, Flòraidh," Algy called, as she vanished into the hole in the peat bank. "Thank you very much."

"That's all very well," snuffled Ruaridh, "but how are you going to find your way to the wood? I can't help you. All I know is that it's somewhere away beyond the Grey Crag."

Ruaridh gestured with his foot, but the mist was so thick that he might as well not have bothered, because there was nothing visible beyond the other side of the Blue Burn. "You'll not be able to see further than your beak on a day like this," Ruaridh continued. "You'll no' find it that way. You'll need to wait while it clears."

"Do you think it will clear by the morning?" Algy asked. "I can't leave it any longer than that, or I will miss the new moon."

"That's a wee problem now, isn't it?" sniffed Ruaridh. "But you'll not see any moon in this either." He sniffed the air thoughtfully, and twitched his whiskers. "Maybe it will lift," he snuffled. "Aye, maybe it will, and maybe it won't. You'll just need to wait and see."

"But you won't tell them I'm going before tomorrow morning, will you?" said Algy.

"Aye, I'll bide my time," sniffed Ruaridh. "But it seems daft to me. There'll be folk at the meeting who know the way to the seven skerries. Why don't you wait and ask them? Maybe some would go with you."

"I'm sure they'll tell me not to go," said Algy. "They think I'm just a silly fluffy bird – a newcomer who doesn't know what he's doing. Good for a song, maybe, but not for something like this!"

"And maybe they're right!" sniffed Ruaridh. "But if your mind is set, you had better go. Just remember... Always alert! Always alert! And keep a sharp lookout over the Grey Crag. That's where you'll find the Laird of the Sky, and you'll no' be a match for him..."

"Who's the Laird of the Sky?" asked Algy nervously.

"Have you not seen him soaring across the bog?" sniffed Ruaridh. "You're a daft bird, to be sure! He's the mighty golden eagle, the true Laird of the Sky. But he'll no' fight you up there. He stoops to the ground to find his prey. Be alert, and if you should see him, fly way up high. You'll be safer there. And if there is nothing else you can do, attack! That's what the crows do, and they always drive him off."

Algy shuddered. "Oh, well," he said, "I suppose there are bound to be dangers. Thank you for the advice! I'll take care, and do my best."

"Well, I think I'll just take a wee nap," snuffled Ruaridh. "I'm not used to all this fuss and bother in the middle of the day. It's no' natural. And I haven't had a good sleep since Plog fell sick."

"Oh, I'm sorry," said Algy. "It must have been a strain for you too, searching for Brianag every day. You have a good rest now. You'll help look after Plog while I'm gone, won't you?"

"That I will," sniffed Ruaridh. "And don't forget, Algy... Always alert!"

"I won't forget," said Algy, giving Ruaridh a very big fluffy hug. "See you soon."

"I'll be seeing you, then," snuffled Ruaridh, rather dubiously, and he turned and hopped in through his doorway in the peat bank.

When his friend had gone, Algy suddenly felt very lonely. He wondered whether he was really doing the right thing in setting out on his own. Perhaps he ought to wait until the meeting the next morning, and consult the others after all.

He was tempted to fly back up to the bog to see Plog again, but with Old Eachann there it might lead to awkward questions. So instead he fluttered across the Blue Burn and down to the sandy beach. A nice stroll on foot might be just what he needed: it would give him time to think things out. Maybe he could ask the sea birds for directions. Many of them travelled long distances, and there would surely be some who knew the way to the seven skerries.

But as Algy trudged along the wet sand, he couldn't see or hear any birds at all; there was no sound on the beach except the sighing of the wind and the slow lapping of the waves on the shore in the dense mist.

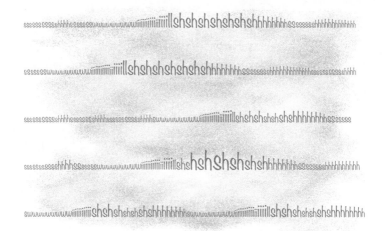

ssssssssssshhhhssssssswwwwwwwwwiiiiiiiiiiiillshshshshshshshhhhhhhhssssssshhhhhhhhhh

ssssssswwwwwwwwwwiiiiiiiiiillshshshshshshshhhhhhhhssssssshhhhhhhhhhhhhhhhhssssssssshhh

ssssssssssshhhhsssssssshhhhssssssssshhhswwwwwwwwwwiiiiiiiiiiiilllshshshshshshhhhhhhhssssss

ssssssssssshhhhssssssswwwwwwwwwwiiiiiiiiiiilllshshshshshshhhhhhhhssssssshhhhhhhhh

swwwwwwwwwwwiiiiiiiiilshshshshshshshhhhhhhhswwwwwwwwwwiiiiiiiiiiilllshshshshshshhhhhhhh

Algy walked slowly along the first beach, across the grassy point in the middle of the bay, and all the way along the big beach, but he didn't meet a single living creature. By the time he had reached his own little beach by the cliffs he was feeling lonelier than ever. There didn't seem to be anyone anywhere who he could turn to for advice or directions. Wondering what to do next, he flew across the rocks to a point that jutted out of the water, not far from his nest, and perched there alone in the drizzling wet mist with the waves swirling all around him.

Staring gloomily at the sullen sea, Algy tried to reason with himself. It was crazy to set off with no idea where he was going. How could he possibly find his way in the mist to a place he had never seen, an uncertain distance away, in a land he didn't know?

The whole plan was absurd. He had no clues to follow except for the hints in the rhymes he had learned from young Flòraidh, and those didn't tell him which direction to take beyond the Grey Crag. It looked as though he would just have to go to the meeting in the morning and ask for help. But that might be too late, or they might prevent him from going... No, it was too risky. He should set off now if he was going to go at all.

As he watched the waves washing the rocks, Algy noticed that the tide was coming in fast. He would have to move very soon, but he still couldn't decide what to do. Perhaps he should go back up to the bog for a while, to see how Plog was getting on now, and maybe talk to Old Eachann. Perhaps the old heron would be willing to help him. Perhaps...

Algy was about to stand up and fly back to the bog when he suddenly spotted the beautiful head of Silvie the seal emerging from the water, just a short distance away from his perch.

"Silvie," he cried. "I'm so glad to see you!"

Ever since the day that Silvie had guided him safely away from the terrible Black Rocks, Algy had thought of her as an extra special friend, although he rarely had a chance to see her. The seal guides were usually much too busy out at sea to linger chatting by the shore, and when they did have time to rest they went to their own home on an island which Algy had never seen. But she was swimming close in to the beach now, and she seemed to be watching him.

As Silvie swam a little nearer to the rocks, she gazed up at Algy gently with her large brown eyes.

"Algyyyyyyyyyyyyyyyyyy," she crooned softly. "Follow meeeeeeeeeeeeeeeeee."

"Are you serious?" said Algy, astonished. "Do you know where I'm going?"

"Algyyyyy, you can follow meeeeeeeeeeeeeeeee" she sang again, and Algy felt sure that her eyes were smiling at him.

"I need to find the Tree with a Golden Heart," Algy said, not at all convinced that Silvie understood the situation. "They say it's somewhere near seven skerries in a silver loch. Do you know where that is?"

"Follow meeeeeeeeeeeeeeeeee," Silvie crooned again. "You'll seeeeeeeeeeeeeeeee."

All of a sudden, a large wave splashed in over Algy's rock and drenched his legs with salty spray. It was time to move! Algy leaped to his feet and up into the air, then hovered there above the rock, looking down at Silvie in the water below him.

"Follow meeeeeeeeeeee. Follow meeeeeeeeeeeeeeeee," Silvie sang again, and turning her head away from the shore, she started to swim out to sea.

## ᴥᴥᴥ Chapter 5 ᴥᴥᴥ
## The Company of Swans

S ilvie the seal swam out into the bay and Algy
flew after her, following as well as he could in the
blurry grey mist. Sometimes Silvie swam just beneath
the surface of the water and Algy was able to see the
shape of her streamlined body quite clearly, so long
as he didn't fly too high. At other times she dived
deeper and it became more difficult to follow, but she
always popped up again before very long, and crooned
"Follow meeeeeeeeeeeeeeee" so that he didn't get lost.

But Algy felt nervous and uneasy flying out to
sea. Since the long and dangerous voyage which had

brought him to this new land, and very nearly drowned him, Algy had avoided flying over the ocean. He was scared that a sudden gust of wind or a huge freak wave would toss him back into the water again, and there wouldn't be a raft to save him the next time. He enjoyed watching and listening to the sea from the safety of the beach, or even from a perch on a large rock in the water, so long as it was close to the shore, but travelling over the waves was another matter entirely. He wondered where Silvie might be taking him, and why, but most of all he just hoped that it wasn't very far.

At first Silvie headed straight out to sea, but she soon swung round to the left and started to swim parallel to the coast. Algy was afraid that she was intending to guide him past the terrible Black Rocks, and for a moment he considered turning back. But then her sleek dark head popped out of the water again, singing "Algyyyyyyyyy, follow meeeeeeeeeeeeeeeeee," and he knew that he had to keep going.

So Algy flew on, keeping as high above the rocky shoals, where the waves churned and crashed, as he could without losing sight of his guide. Before long, Silvie turned again, and Algy was relieved to see that she was swimming in towards the land, at a spot where low growing birch trees and hazel bushes covered the sloping hillside right down to a narrow beach of pale sand, which was framed by rugged piles of rock sticking out into the sea on either side.

Algy was surprised to see a small company of beautiful white swans in this tiny bay. Some of them were floating on the water, close in to the shore, and others were paddling about at the edge of the beach, feeding among the masses of seaweed exposed by the low tide, or exploring the burn that trickled across the sand into the sea. Silvie paused and looked up at Algy with her big brown eyes. "Algyyyyyyyyyy," she sang. "Algyyyyyyyyyy. Here is some companyyyyyyyyyyyyyy. Theyyyyy are going your wayyyyyyyyy."

Algy was astonished. "You mean the swans can take me to the seven skerries?" he called to her in amazement.

"Follow the companyyyyyyyyyyyyyyyyy," she crooned. "Follow the companyyyyyyyyyyyyyyyy."

"Thank you!" cried Algy, although he still didn't understand how Silvie could know where he was going. "Thank you very much!"

"I hope you find the treeeeeeeeeeeee," crooned Silvie, and she dived beneath the water and vanished.

Algy remained hovering in the air for a few moments more, to see whether Silvie would surface again, but there was no further sign of her, so he flew towards the beach and landed on solid ground with a sigh of relief.

The swans were large, impressive birds, and although their feathers were white like his own, they were not fluffy, but wonderfully sleek and elegant in a way that Algy knew he could never be. He felt a little overawed in the company of such beautiful creatures, and at first he could not think of anything to say.

The swans swayed their long, arching necks gracefully at him, and called out softly in tuneful, whooping voices, "Whoo whoo whoo whoooo, Algy, how are yooou?" A single swan called first, and then several others joined in until there was quite a chorus, all calling "Whoo whoo whoo whoooo, Algy, how do you dooooo? Whoo whoo whoo whoooo, Algy, how are yooou?"

Algy was startled to find that the swans knew his name, but it had been such a strange day altogether that he was not as surprised as he might have been. "Ummm, how do you do?" he said politely. "I'm very pleased to meet you."

"Whoo whoo whoo whoooo, Algy, whoo whoo whoo whoooo. We are pleased tooooo," called the swans.

Algy fluttered closer to the edge of the water and perched on one of the many rocks that stuck out of the sand. "I need to find a very special place," he said hesitantly, looking shyly from one swan to another. "It's a place where they say there are seven skerries in a silver loch, near a shore with ancient woodland which contains the Tree with a Golden Heart. I don't suppose you know where that might be, do you?"

"Whoo whoo whoo whoooo, yes we dooooo. Whoo whoo whoo whoooo, yes we dooooo. Algy we can help yooou. Whoo whoo whoo whoo whoooo!"

"You know where it is?" Algy cried eagerly. "You can take me there?"

"True, true, we dooooo, whoo whoo whoo whoooooo, we're travelling throoough," called the swans. "We'll fly with yooou. We'll fly with yooou."

"That's wonderful!" exclaimed Algy. "Thank you so much!"

The swans who had been foraging at the edge of the beach paddled into the sea to join their floating friends, and they all milled around together, dipping their long necks down beneath the water, to pick up some last morsels from the seaweed beds. Then they started to nod and bob their heads, calling quietly to one another in their whooping voices.

Suddenly, the whole company of swans lifted their bodies and began to run awkwardly across the surface of the sea, with one large, handsome swan out in front. Their webbed feet flap-flapped against the water as they tried to lift off, and their enormous wings flapped too, in a beautiful rhythmical swooping motion.

Algy had never watched a company of swans taking off from the sea before, and he was surprised at how much difficulty they seemed to have, although it was a magnificent sight. But in a few moments more they were all in the air, and they turned and called down to him, "Whoo whoo whoo whoo whoooo. Now yooou, Algy, now yooou."

Without waiting for him to join them, the swans immediately started to fly inland, rising higher in the sky with every beat of their powerful wings. Algy leaped into the air and flew rapidly after them, anxious to catch up before they vanished into the mist. But following a company of swans was a very different matter from following a seal, and Algy had to fly as hard and as fast as he could. He was quite out of breath by the time that he reached them, and he was relieved to be able to settle into the slipstream behind the great birds in front.

"Whoo whoo whoo whoooo, Algy, how are yooou?" the swans called, their huge wings beating rhythmically the entire time with a continual whooshing, swishing noise. "We'll fly with yooou. We'll fly with yooou."

"Thank you," gasped Algy, still flapping vigorously and struggling to catch his breath as the whole company swept on rapidly through the mist. "Thank you."

From time to time, one of the swans at the front of the V formation dropped back to join him, calling "Whoo whoo whoo whoooo, Algy, how are yooou?" when it took its place by his side. But most of the time they just flew on steadily in a synchronized rhythm of wingbeats, whooping continuously to each other as though Algy was not there, and he just did his best to keep up.

As they travelled further inland, the mist grew patchier and Algy could see the hillsides around him, although not the ridges at their tops, as those were still covered by dense low clouds. Little wisps of mist seemed to have broken away from the big masses of cloud above them, and were drifting across the lower parts of the steep slopes on their own. Algy imagined that the wisps were setting out on an adventure, just like he was, and as he watched them drift by he began to feel more and more excited at the thought of exploring a new part of the land which was now his home.

The beautiful white swans swept on into the unknown and Algy's spirits soared as they climbed ever higher into the sky. He felt thrilled to be flying with them, and the fact that he didn't know what lay ahead just added to his excitement.

When they entered the thick cloud over the first high ridge, Algy remembered Ruaridh's warning about the Laird of the Sky. It was impossible to see anything much inside the cloud, and he began to feel nervous. But then he glanced at the swans in front of him and realized that he was not likely to be in any danger, so long as he kept close to them. Perhaps one swan alone might not be a match for a mighty eagle, but no creature would risk interfering with a whole company of swans, especially if they became angry.

Inside the cloud he could no longer see where he was going, but the swans did not hesitate or interrupt their flight for a moment. Algy guessed that they were passing over several different ridges, because he occasionally caught glimpses of craggy peaks of bare, wet rock below, but it was impossible to get an impression of the landscape as a whole. It seemed to be very rugged and quite mountainous, although, from the feel of the air, he didn't think that they were climbing terribly high.

From time to time the company passed through thinner areas of cloud and Algy got a better view. Looking down, he saw large stretches of drab, brown moorland and patches of dense, dark forest. For a few moments, away on the left, he could see a hint of the ocean, flat and grey in the distance, but it was much too misty to see any islands, so it provided no clue to where he was.

After a while they emerged into clearer air and started to fly along the length of a narrow inland loch. It lay calm and black beneath them, at the bottom of a deep valley with forest on each side, and Algy tried to make a mental note of what it looked like. He knew that it was going to be difficult to find his way back on his own, when he had seen so little on the outward flight, so he made an effort to remember every notable feature of the landscape.

When they reached the far end of the loch, the swans swept through a pass between two grassy hillsides that rose into the clouds, and as the company flew on, the land fell away in front of them, into a wide, bowl-shaped area of moorland lying between the hills. Algy thought he caught a glimpse of more water ahead, and sure enough, as they passed over the far end of the moor and dropped down lower again, he could see a large expanse of silver in a distinctive half-moon bay, fringed with a sandy beach, at the foot of a steep but grassy mountainside.

The swans began to descend towards a flat area of grass at the back of the beach. As the company approached the ground they all put their legs down and started running with their big webbed feet in a wobbly, awkward sort of way. It seemed to be almost as hard for them to land as to take off, and Algy was glad that he could land and jump into the air without that kind of difficulty, even if he couldn't fly like a swan.

As soon as they had all touched down, the swans started milling about again, pecking at the ground. "Whoo whoo whoo whoooo, Algy, how are yooou?" they called to him. "Whoo whoo whoo whoooooo, won't you eat something toooo?" But there was nothing for Algy to eat in the grass, so he just perched on one side and waited while the swans browsed around. The mist was continuing to lift, and he could see now that the water stretched out in front of him from left to right, and there was more land on the other side.

"Is this the silver loch?" he asked one of the swans nearest to him. "Whooo, whooo, the silver loch, that's truuuue," answered the swan. "We'll fly with yooou. We'll fly with yooou."

Suddenly the swans started nodding and bobbing their heads at each other again, and in a moment or two more they began to run clumsily across the grass, their feet slapping the turf from side to side as they tried to lift off. They had even more difficulty taking off from the ground than from the sea, but eventually they all returned to the sky, and Algy jumped back into the air to follow them. The company circled to the left, heading out a little way from the land, and then started to fly along the silver loch.

The swans swept on, calling to each other and to Algy, and once again he stayed close behind them, doing his best to keep up. They flew so fast that he didn't have much time to observe what lay below, but as they kept following the loch, he guessed that it would be simple to find his way back, for this part of the journey at least.

It was getting very late in the day now, and the light was beginning to grow dim. Algy was just starting to wonder how much further they were going to travel before nightfall when two of the swans called out to him. "Whoo whoo whoo whoooo, Algy how are yooou? We must leave yooou, whooo, whoooo; we're travelling throoough, whoo whoo whoo whooooooo."

"Do you mean that this is the place I'm looking for?" Algy called back to them, excitedly.

"Truuue, truuue, whooo whooooooo," some of them answered, without breaking the rhythm of their flight. "The place for yooou, whoo whoo whoo whoooo."

Algy looked down. He could see quite a lot of little islands in the loch; too many to count easily. The shoreline on the near side of the water was jagged and irregular, with numerous rocky inlets, and the hillsides above it were all covered with trees at the lower levels. There was no one spot that clearly matched the description in the rhyme he had learned from young Flòraidh.

The swans did not alter their pace, and Algy realized that they were already beginning to fly past the place where he ought to land.

"Oh, I must go!" he cried. "I'm so sorry to leave you! You've been so kind. Thank you, thank you! I hope I see you again."

"Whoo whoo whoo whoooo, we're sorry too, Algy. But we're travelling throooough, whooo, whooo; we'll see yoooou. We'll see yoooou, whoo whoo whoo whoooo."

Algy started to drop down in the air away from them, and suddenly the whole company of swans called out to him together in their tuneful, whooping voices, while they continued to fly onwards with their huge wings still maintaining their constant, rhythmic beat. "Whoo whoo whoo whoooo, Algy, we'll see yoooou. We'll see yoooou, Algy, whoo whoo whoo whoooo."

"I hope I'll see you again soon!" Algy called back to them, as he remained hovering in the air, watching the swans fly away. "Thank you again! Have a safe journey!"

"Whoo whoo whoo whoooo, Algy, we'll see yoooou. Whoo whoo whoo whoooo, Algy," they continued to call, but their voices grew fainter and fainter, and very soon the huge birds looked like nothing more than little dots disappearing into the sky.

Sadly, Algy dropped down through the air and landed on a small, rocky island immediately below him, close to the shore of the silver loch. He suddenly felt very lonely again. Not only had he lost the company of the beautiful swans, but he was in a strange new place, without any friends, and without any clear idea of where to find the Tree with a Golden Heart. He wasn't even sure that he could find his way home.

However, the light was fading fast. He could do nothing more that evening except look for a safe place to sleep.

Algy was glad that he had landed on an island, as it was likely to be safer from the fierce animals of the night than the mainland, but it had little to offer by way of comfort. The ground was mainly bare rock, exposed and cold, with occasional patches of very thin, scrubby grass. But a few trees and low bushes had rooted here and there, in hollows in the stone, and they were dominated by one tall stand of pine trees. With their long, straight trunks leading up to dense, spreading crowns, the pines offered plenty of protection, so although he was used to sleeping on a cosy bed of dried leaves and heather flowers, Algy decided to spend this night on a perch, as far away as possible from the unknown dangers on the ground.

Settling on a strong branch near the top of the highest pine tree, Algy made himself as comfortable as he could, with his back pressed against the rough bark of the trunk, and tried to go to sleep, wondering what the next day would bring.

As he dozed on and off, he was happy to hear the sound of little waves lapping softly against the rocky shore of the island below. The mist had been so thick that he had not realized the silver loch was a sea loch. Algy was comforted by the thought that he was still connected with his home in the Bay of the Sand Islands, and although the sound was much quieter and more gentle than the pounding of the wild ocean waves on the beach and rocks beside his cliff-side home, it provided a reassuring lullaby to help him fall asleep in this unfamiliar place...

lap-lap lapplapplap lapple-lap-lap-lap lappleapplap-lapple lap-lap-lap-lapple-applaplapple lap-lap-lap lapplaplap lappleap-plap-lapple lap-lap-lap lapple-app lap-lapple lap-lap-lap lapple-app-lap-lapple lap-lap-lap-lapple lap-lap-lap-lap lap-lap-lap-lapple-app lapppp lap-lap lapplapplap lapple-lap-lap-lap lap-lap-lap-lap lap-lap-lap-lapple-app lapppp lappleapplap-lapple lap-lap-lap-lapple-applaplapple lapple-lap-lap-lap lapple-lap-lap-lap lap-lap-lap lapplaplap lap lap-lap-lap-lap lapple-applaplapple lapple-lap-lap-lap lapple-app lap-lapple lap-lap-lap lap-lap-lap lap-lap-lap-lapple-app lapppp lap-lap lap-lap-lap-lap lap-lap-lap-lapple-app lapppp lap-lap

## ≈≋ Chapter 6 ≋≈
## The Trickling of the Hidden Burn

Algy woke up early the next morning, just as the dawn sky was beginning to show the first pale hints of daylight. For a moment he thought he must still be asleep and dreaming, as everything around him seemed so strange and new. He was apparently on a rough perch, high up in a pine tree on a small rocky island, and he could dimly see the shore of a land he didn't recognize, very close by. Rubbing his eyes, Algy peered at the landscape again, and gradually he began to remember. The company of beautiful white swans had brought him to this place on the silver loch and flown on without him, leaving him here on his own to find the Tree with a Golden Heart.

The sky was bright and clear, and it looked as though it was going to be a fine day. The morning star was still twinkling prettily, close to the ridge on the other side of the loch, and the air was fragrant with the smell of pine needles and resin. Algy took lots of slow, deep breaths and began to feel a little stronger. Glancing around, he noticed a small, weatherbeaten rowan tree, growing in a pocket in the rock. It had already lost most of its orange berries, but there were still enough left for a light breakfast. So he hopped down to the rowan, ate what he could, then dropped to the ground and splashed himself vigorously with water from a shallow rainwater pool that had formed in a hollow nearby.

Algy was not at all sure what to do next. He thought about the rhyme he had memorized:

"It's said that the Tree with a Golden Heart
In the ancient oak wood stands apart,
Near the point where the forest meets the shore
And overhead the eagles soar;
The hillside there climbs steep and high
To barren summits in the sky,
But the brae is clothed in oak and birch,
And at its foot is the place to search,
For the entrance to the wood is found
Where silver loch meets rocky ground
Near seven skerries, bleak and black."

Algy looked around. He couldn't see a group of seven skerries, although there were many small islands of odd shapes and sizes scattered across the loch, and some of them were bleak and black. The forest appeared to meet the shore all the way along the lochside, every hill he could see was steep and high, and almost all the summits were bare. That wasn't much help!

He peered at the woodland across the water. There were plenty of massive oak trees near the shore, and some clumps of silver birches too. Here and there, stands of tall pine trees like the one he had slept in reached up towards the sky, but that was no help either, as the rhyme didn't mention pines at all. And there was bare rock at every point where the land met the silver loch, except in the small, seaweedy bay immediately in front of him, which had a shingle beach. It looked as though almost any spot he might choose would match the description in the verses as well as any other. He had to find the Tree with a Golden Heart before the end of the day... but how?

Algy was entirely flummoxed. The company of swans had seemed quite certain they had brought him to the right place, but it was possible that he had flown on with them too far, and should have landed sooner. In that case it was most unlikely that the Tree with a Golden Heart was further up the loch, so perhaps he should fly back a little way, in the direction he had come, to see whether he could find the seven skerries there.

Algy had just begun to recite the rhyme once more, to make sure that he hadn't missed any clues, when he suddenly heard a strange voice.

"What, what, what, what, what?" it squawked. "What have we here?"

It sounded rather like the voice of a large sea bird, and yet not quite like a bird. Algy peered at the rocks in front of him, and at the little islands nearby, but he couldn't see any bird at all. Then he noticed a shiny brown shape slinking across the mass of seaweed at the tideline where the rocks met the water. It wasn't a bird, it was an animal, and it was all wet.

"Hello!" Algy exclaimed in surprise.

"Hello yourself," squawked the animal. "And who might you be?"

"I'm Algy," said Algy. "I'm a fluffy bird."

"Is that so?" squawked the strange animal. "If you're a bird, you're a very peculiar one! How come I've never seen you before? Did you drop out of the sky, maybe? Was it raining fluffy birds last night?" and the odd creature chuckled at its own joke, scattering drops of water everywhere as it shook with laughter.

Looking more closely, Algy observed that the animal was dripping all over, and its brown coat was soaked and streaked into gleaming, triangular clumps of fur in a most unusual way. At the back it had a long, wide, strangely shaped tail like a paddle, and at the front it had plenty of very sharp teeth. He began to feel rather nervous, and hastily jumped up into a bush that was growing close to the rocky shore of the island.

"Now what did you do that for?" squawked the animal sulkily. "That's not very friendly-like."

"Ummm, well..." Algy hesitated, feeling a little embarrassed. "I didn't mean to be rude, but I don't know what kind of creature you are, and I thought maybe you might like to eat fluffy birds!"

"That's a good one!" laughed the creature. "Don't know what kind of creature I am! Well, I never! Where've you been all your life?" and it laughed again, shaking so vigorously that a spray of sparkling water flew up and sprinkled Algy in his bush.

"I'm sorry," said Algy. "But I haven't been in this land very long, and I haven't met all the creatures that live here yet."

"You don't say!" squawked the animal. "So you really did drop out of the sky!"

"Well, I only came to this place yesterday, with a company of swans," said Algy, "and then I did drop out of the sky, I suppose. But I originally arrived in this land by sea. On a raft. That was a little while ago now. But who are you?"

"I'm Ailsa the otter," squawked the animal, "as if you didn't know! But don't you worry! I don't eat birds if I can help it!"

"If you can help it!" exclaimed Algy, horrified, and he shot back up to the top of the pine tree he had slept in. "What if you can't help it?" he called down to the creature below.

"There are plenty of fish in the loch," squawked the otter, laughing again. "You don't need to fly up your tree in a huff!"

"Are you sure?" asked Algy, fearing a trick.

"I've had my breakfast today!" squawked the otter, looking up at Algy mischievously, and it rubbed its tummy with one of its front feet.

Algy was alarmed to see that it had extremely long, pointed claws. "I hope you have!" he said with some feeling. "But I think maybe I'll stay in this tree, if you don't mind. I don't want to be rude, but I don't want to be breakfast either... or lunch!"

The otter chuckled again. "You're a droll one, to be sure," she squawked. "But I really don't want to eat you. I don't like feathers!"

Algy thought it was high time to change the subject. "Do you live here?" he asked.

"Certainly," squawked the otter. "What else would I be doing here at this time of the morning?"

"Well I don't live here, but I'm here now," said Algy, and he started to laugh too. It didn't look as though the otter could climb a tree – not with that paddle tail – so he began to calm down and relax. "I wonder whether you could help me, then?" he said.

"Help you with what?" asked the otter. "With your breakfast?" And it laughed again.

"Let's not think any more about breakfast," said Algy. "I need to find a particular tree, to help my friend who has been very ill. It's called the Tree with a Golden Heart. I don't suppose you know where it is?"

"Never heard of it," squawked the otter. "Tree with a golden what?"

"A golden heart," said Algy. "There's a special rhyme that describes where to find it." And he recited the rhyme again, to the otter.

"I'm not that good at counting," squawked the otter, "so I can't tell about the skerries, though there's plenty of them here!" She waved her paddle tail at the rocky islands surrounding them. "And I don't know any cloven tree," she continued. "But there's a hidden burn with a waterfall, up among the oak trees around the next point. I often go up there myself." This time she pointed her tail the other way, in the direction the swans had flown after Algy had left them. "It's not far from the loch."

"Thank you," said Algy. "That's very helpful."

"But there are many burns in the woods," the otter went on. "The hillsides are that steep, the water is bound to fall down them." She laughed again. "And most of them are hidden."

"I suppose so," said Algy, discouraged.

"Your rhyme doesn't sound much good to me," squawked the otter. "But I wish you luck, if you're trying to help your friend. That's a fine thing, to help a friend!" And without another word she swivelled round, bounded across the rock, and slid into the loch.

"Thank you!" Algy called again.

The otter paused with her head sticking out of the water, and looked back at him. "And don't forget about breakfast!" she squawked, chuckling again, then dived underneath and disappeared.

Algy stared at the densely wooded hillsides. Without any more information, it was going to be exceedingly difficult to find the right place. It would take far too long to search the woods thoroughly, and the chances of finding the tree that way were slim in any case. So the only sensible options were to fly up and down the loch in the hope of spotting the seven skerries, or to go and look for the otter's hidden burn in the wood.

It was still very early in the morning, so there was plenty of time to do both, but one lay in one direction and one lay in the other. Which should he try first? He thought and thought and thought and thought... and finally decided to try the otter's burn. He was almost certain that it lay in the wrong direction and would turn out to be a waste of time, but it wouldn't take long just to fly round the corner and have a peek, and if the tree was not there he could spend the rest of the day searching in the other direction.

Algy jumped into the air and flew over the rocky point that jutted out into the loch. There was another little inlet beyond the point, and a burn was trickling out into the loch there, across a small, flat marshy area by the shore. But Algy had lived in this new land long enough to know that every inlet and bay would be sure to have at least one burn running across it, carrying the rainwater from the hills down into the lochs and the sea, so he didn't get too excited.

Landing on the sodden grass at the back of the inlet, Algy looked at the woods. Most of the trees were oaks, but there was no sign of any cloven tree. There was no path leading from the shore either, so it didn't look very promising, but Algy flew into the woodland nevertheless, following the line of the burn as closely as he could.

The further Algy advanced into the wood, the more sure he became that this was not the place described in the rhyme. He was just about to give up and return to the loch when he noticed a small waterfall up ahead, splashing prettily into a round pool. He hadn't really had a proper bath that morning, nor a good drink of clean water, so he decided to rest there briefly and refresh himself. There were also some brambles growing nearby: a few juicy ripe blackberries would complete his breakfast very nicely!

It was pleasant splashing about in the edge of the woodland pool with the delicious taste of blackberries in his mouth, and the burn water tasted lovely too, so when he hauled himself out onto a mossy rock to dry, Algy was feeling much more relaxed.

He settled back and looked at the scene around him. Above the far side of the pool the burn tumbled down the steep hill in a series of little waterfalls carved out of the underlying rock, with many dainty ferns and other plants growing by its edges. Then it splashed merrily into the pool in a shower of bubbles and white spray, and swirled around and around in circles before continuing on its course towards the loch. There were several large boulders beside the edge of the pool, with soft coverings of thick moss, and bright rays of sunlight were filtering through the gaps between the leaves of the great oak trees which towered above him, creating pretty patterns of light and shadow on the water and the surrounding plants. Altogether it was a lovely spot in which to rest, and very different from anything Algy had seen near his home in the Bay of the Sand Islands.

In fact, it was so peaceful in the woodland, with the gentle rustling of the breeze through the leaves, and the soothing sound of the little waterfall and trickling burn, that although he intended to move on and search for the seven skerries without delay, Algy started to doze. He had not slept well on his perch in the pine tree, and he was still exhausted from all the days and nights spent beside Plog's sickbed, not to mention his energetic flight with the swans.

So, as he listened to the water trickling and gurgling and splashing around him, Algy's head slowly began to nod...

Tweetle tweetle tweetie tweet ♫ ♫ ♫♩ Here's a treat, a bird with big feet sang a lovely voice. Tweetie tweet, what splendid feet ♫♩ But I think the bird is fast asleep. Fast asleep, fast asleep, tweetie tweet, he's fast asleep ♫ ♩

Algy woke up with a start. "That's not very polite!" he said. "I heard what you sang about my feet."

Tweetie tweet, I'm sorry, I'm sure ♩ ♫ ♩ ♩ sang the robin, who was perching on a branch that hung low over the pool, just a short distance away from Algy. Tweetie tweet ♪♩ I'll not sing any more.

"Oh, that's all right," said Algy. "Please don't stop singing. My feet really are large, but nobody mentions it as a rule. I'm very glad to see you, really I am."

Tweetie tweetie tweetle tweet ♫ ♪ ◡ ♩ That's fine, that's fine, the pleasure is mine, sang the robin. Tweetie tweet, the pleasure is mine ♫ ♩ ♩

"Mine too," said Algy. "I'm always happy to meet a robin." Suddenly he noticed that the sun wasn't shining through the leaves any more; the light had almost faded away. "Gracious!" he gasped. "How long have I slept? What time of day is it now?"

Tweetie tweet, the sun slips away, the sun slips away at the end of the day. ♫ ♩♫ ♩ Time for a song, it's time for a song, perhaps you would like to sing along? ♫♩ ♫♫♩♩ Tweetie tweet, tweetie tweet, tweetle tweetle tweetie tweet.

"The end of the day!" exclaimed Algy. "Oh, no! How can that have happened? It was early morning just a short time ago."

Tweetie tweet ♫♩ You slept all day, there's no time left to sing and play, sang the robin.

"Slept all day!" cried Algy desperately. "But I've got to find the Tree with a Golden Heart before the new moon sinks down in the gloaming."

Tweetie tweetle tweetie tweet, why do that when we can chat? ♫ ♪ ♩ Tweetie tweet ♫♩ Have a nice chat?

"You don't understand," Algy said miserably, "I've got to find the tree right now! My friend has been ill,

84

and I have to sleep in the Tree with a Golden Heart and wait for a guide to help me find three lichens. It has to be on the night when I first see the new moon sinking down."

The robin whistled Tweeeeeeeeeeeeeeeeeeeet ♫♫♫♪♫♫♪ Tweetie tweetie tweet ♫ ♫♩ Your friend has been ill? ♫ What's the matter? Did he take a chill?

"He was very ill indeed," said Algy. "He had the bog fever, and he lay for days and days without moving or doing anything. The fever went away in the end, but now his mind is damaged. I've come here to collect some special medicine for him. I have to find the three old lichens of the bark, to make a crottle porridge."

Tweetie tweetie tweetle tweeeeeeeeeet ♫♫ ♫ ♩ exclaimed the robin. Is that really so? Then off we go ♩♫♩ Off we go, if that's really so. Tweetie tweetie tweetle tweet, off we go, don't be slow ♩♫ ♩♫

"You don't mean you know where the tree is!" cried Algy in great excitement. "Do you really? Do you know where it is?"

Tweetie tweet ♫♩ That ancient tree is one I very often see ♫ ♫ ♩ Tweetie tweetle, follow me; follow me to that special tree ♫♩ ♫ ♫ ♩

"I will!" cried Algy, "I will! Lead the way!"

The robin hopped up onto another branch above Algy's head, and then fluttered up and up again, rising higher and higher through the trees from branch to branch. Algy sometimes lost sight of his little guide, but when he reached the highest branches he saw the

85

robin waiting patiently, right at the top of a tall oak tree. Algy joined him as fast as he could, and looked out over the treetops. From there they could see the silver loch, but it was no longer silver. The sun was setting, and the surface of the loch was reflecting all the beautiful gold and red colours of the sunset.

"The sun's going down!" cried Algy in alarm. "I'll never make it in time."

*Tweetle tweetie tweetle tweet ♫ ♪ ♩ ♩ Oh yes you will! Oh yes you will! Tweetle tweetie tweet ♫ ♪ ♩ ♩ It's only just beyond the hill!*

The robin flew up into the air and Algy followed him, back in the direction he had come with the swans. They passed over the tops of countless trees, with the rocky peaks of the hills rising high on their right-hand side and the beautiful glowing loch on their left. Algy spotted the island he had landed on the night before, and the little seaweedy bay that lay close to it, but the robin didn't stop there. He flew on over another patch of woodland which rose up a hillside beyond the little bay, and then began to sweep down towards the ground.

The sunset sky was beginning to change colour now, from yellow-gold and orangey-red to a deep crimson, and Algy knew that he had very little time left to find the tree. "Is it here?" he gasped, as he followed the robin into the top of another oak tree. Most of the trees near the loch seemed to be oaks, and he could not see much difference between them, although each one had its own distinctive shape.

*Tweetle tweet ♫♩ You'll see, you'll see,* sang the robin, fluttering down through the branches to the ground.

There were many areas of moss-covered rock on the woodland floor, surrounded by a deep carpet of old, dry leaves that rustled when Algy touched them. Green ferns and bracken were growing between the rocks, and there were even some patches of late-flowering heather, although the bushes had grown unnaturally thin and straggly beneath the tall trees. Algy was excited to see that in this wood there was indeed a narrow deer track, which led up the hill from the loch. The robin fluttered ahead a little way, following this track as he hopped in short flights from one mossy stone to another, then he stopped to sing again.

*Tweetle tweetle tweetie tweet ♫ ♫ ♫ ♩ Listen to the sounds you hear, a trickling burn is flowing near ♩ ♫ ♩ Tweetle tweetle tweetie tweet ♫ ♫ ♫ ♩*

Algy listened carefully. The robin was right. He could hear a loud trickling sound, but he could see no sign of the burn. The words of the rhyme came back to him:

> "The deer have made a muddy track:
>   Ascend this path until you hear
>   The sound of water running near;
>   The trickling of the hidden burn
>   Is loudest at the point to turn.
>   Then, looking back at what you passed
>   You'll see the cloven tree at last."

Quickly, Algy turned round and looked back down the path... and there it was! It had two separate trunks which grew out of the ground a little distance apart, leaning away from each other before arching together to form an open heart at the base of a massive tree. After the two sides joined, a single trunk rose up towards the sky until eventually it split apart again, each side with its own branches reaching outwards and upwards. Algy had never seen any tree like it before.

As he gazed in wonder, the last rays of the setting sun shot through the woodland and flooded the arched area between the two trunks with a warm, golden light. He had found the Tree with a Golden Heart!

"Thank you, thank you, thank you!" Algy cried to the robin. "I'd like to give you the fluffiest hug, but you're too small! But I thank you with all my heart!"

Tweetle tweetle tweetie tweet ♫ ♫ ♫ ♩ Take care, take care, now that you're here ♩ ♩ ♩ ♩

"Yes, I know about the dangers," said Algy. "But it's the time of the gloaming and I must enter the tree at once, or it will be too late."

Tweetie tweet, this ancient tree, you must treat most respectfully ♫ ♩ ♩ ♫ ♪ Take care, take care, beware, beware! ♩ ♩ Tweetie tweetle tweetie tweet.

"I'll be careful," said Algy. "Somehow I just know that I'll be all right. Will I see you in the morning?"

Tweetie tweet ♫ ♩ We'll see, we'll see. Sleep well inside that strange old tree ♩ ♫ ♩ Tweetie tweet, sweet dreams

88

tonight ♪♫ I hope that you don't get a fright! And with that the robin flitted off through the trees in the twilight, and vanished among the leaves.

"Good night," Algy called after him. "Sweet dreams!"

Algy fluttered slowly over to the remarkable tree and perched on a boulder in front of it. He thought hard, trying to recall the exact words of the second rhyme that young Flòraidh had taught him.

"In the gloaming, not before,
  Enter through the heather door,
  Then, as the crescent moon sinks low,
  Close your eyes in its pale glow;
  Prepare yourself for slumber deep,
  Repeat these lines until you sleep."

Algy looked at the open arch between the two trunks. A straggly heather bush was growing just in front of it – a strange, tall, bedraggled sort of plant which stretched out across the entrance to the heart of the tree. That must be the door! Very carefully, Algy stepped up to the bush and gently moved the thin twiggy branches aside. Then, feeling both excited and nervous at the same time, he stepped softly into the heart of the tree. The space was just tall enough for him to stand up in.

Once he was inside the tree, Algy found that he was able to see out of the other side. On the far side of the tree the hillside fell away, down towards the loch, and although there were other trees growing lower down the slope, their branches were not dense; he could see the shimmering water of the loch with its sunset reflections quite clearly. The sun had sunk below the hills on the far side of the loch now, and the colours had changed from crimson-red to the soft violet of the gloaming. As Algy looked up, he suddenly saw the new moon: a lovely bright crescent in the darkening sky, hanging low above a long, shadowy ridge. A sparkle of light lower down caught his eye too, and he realized that the new moon was reflected in the water of the loch. It was a beautiful scene, but also a sign that he must prepare himself to sleep without delay.

Looking one last time at the crescent moon, Algy curled himself up on the dry leaves which covered the ground in the heart of the tree, closed his eyes, and quietly chanted the special lines which Flòraidh had taught him:

"Golden heart of the ancient tree,
  Send a trusty guide to me."

He repeated the rhyme softly, over and over again, until the sky grew entirely dark, and until he could repeat it no more, for he had fallen fast asleep.

## ꙮ Chapter 7 ꙮ
## The Tree with a Golden Heart

Very, very slowly, Algy opened one eye half way, then the other, and hastily shut them both again. He was sure it was the middle of the night, but he seemed to be surrounded by a strange golden glow.

Gingerly, he tried opening his eyes once more, just a teeny-weeny bit, and peeked out through a tiny crack between his eyelashes. There was no doubt about it: he was lying in a pool of bright golden light. It didn't look like sunlight and it didn't look like moonlight. In fact, it didn't look like any kind of light he had ever seen before.

Closing his eyes again, Algy listened carefully, keeping absolutely still in case there was something dangerous out there which might notice him if he moved. The trees of the woodland were creaking quietly, and the dry leaves on the ground were rustling a little in the breeze, but he couldn't hear any other sound except the distant trickling of the hidden burn as it made its way down the wooded hillside to the loch below. There was no hint of any creature moving about, and no explanation for the weird golden light.

Algy plucked up his courage. After all, there was not necessarily any cause for alarm, and he had certainly not come this far just to turn coward when something peculiar occurred. Indeed, he had been hoping that something special would happen.

Taking a deep breath to calm his nerves, he opened his eyes fully and looked around. The heart of the tree was filled with the remarkable golden light, but the woodland beyond it was entirely dark. He tried to peep through the heather door, but there was nothing out there except velvety blackness, made even darker by the contrast with the light inside. Algy was amazed, but the golden light had a lovely warm glow to it, and somehow it made him feel happy.

"Is anybody there?" he whispered, turning his head this way and that.

The night wind murmured through the autumn leaves on the woodland trees, but that was all.

"Is anybody there?" he whispered again into the darkness, with the tip of his beak poking out through the thin twigs of the heather door, but there was no answer.

Algy lay back on the cosy little bed of dried leaves in the heart of the tree and let the golden glow bathe him with its warmth. He felt strangely comfortable and drowsy, but there was obviously something extraordinary about the situation, and although he was very tired, he thought that he should stay awake. Of course it was possible that he was not awake at all, but still asleep and dreaming. Some dreams could be surprisingly convincing. Algy tried biting himself to see if it hurt. It certainly did! He reached up and brushed his wing lightly against one trunk of the divided tree: the bark felt rough and real.

As he touched the tree, another part of the rhyme he had learned from young Flòraidh came into his mind.

"And when you see the shining light,
 Be not startled, take no fright.
 State your purpose, clear and true,
 And then a guide will come to you."

Algy felt foolish and rather nervous about talking out loud inside the glowing heart of a tree in the middle of the night, especially as there didn't seem to be anyone around to hear what he said. But he knew he would have to explain his reason for being there if he wanted someone to help him, so, hoping that if there was anyone out there they would be friendly, Algy started to speak.

"Hello," he said quietly. "Hello. I'm Algy. A fluffy bird. I've come to ask for help."

He paused, half afraid and half hoping that he would hear some response which would encourage him to go on, but although he listened for the slightest hint of a voice, he could still hear nothing except the normal night-time noises of the woodland around him.

Feeling even more foolish, Algy continued, although he didn't believe that anyone was listening.

"My special friend, Plog the frog, has been terribly ill," he went on. "He caught the bog fever and lay sick in his bed for many, many days. We couldn't do much for him, and we didn't know whether he would get better. In the end, the fever did go away, and he is out of danger now, but he is still not right at all. He's very weak and sickly, but the worst thing is that his mind is damaged. He's not himself any more. Plog was a poet: they called him the Bard of the Bog. But now he has lost his sense of rhyme. He still tries to make up verses, but they don't rhyme, and often they don't even make sense. I don't think he understands much that we say to him, either. Poor Plog!"

Algy sighed, and listened again, but still there was no reply.

"Poor Plog," Algy murmured sadly again. "He used to be so lively and witty and smart. It was such fun making up rhymes with him! But now he's just muddled and confused. He has lost interest in everything. Everything is wrong." Algy stopped, realizing that he was starting to talk to himself.

He tried to peer outside the tree, but nothing had changed. There was only a velvety blackness beyond the heather door, and not a sign that anyone could hear him. Making one last effort, Algy spoke out as loudly as he could, in case whoever might be out there was not very close by.

"Can you please help me help my friend Plog?" he almost shouted. "They say there are lichens in this wood which could cure his mind, but I don't know which they are, or where to find them. Can you please help me find them? Please!"

"Whhur WoooOOOooooo. Whhurr Wwww Wwww Wwwww wOOOouoooooooo."

Algy leaped with fright and hit his head on the arch of the tree trunk above him.

"Wwww Wwww Wwwww oOOouoooooooo, Wwww Wwww Wwwwwo OOouoooooooo."

"Oh, it's only an owl," Algy gasped, rubbing his sore head with his wing.

"OOOOooooooooooooooowWwwwoooooooOO. OOOOoooooooooowWwoooOOOO."

"Are you the guide who will help me?" Algy called out through the glowing doorway, into the darkness.

He heard the swish of an owl's wings swooping past, but he did not get any reply.

"Shall I follow you? I can't see where you are."

"Wwww Wwww Wwwww OOouoooo," hooted the owl. "OOOOoooo Wwww Wwww Www WOoooooo."

Standing up carefully inside the tree, Algy gently moved some of the twiggy branches of the straggly heather bush aside and leaned through the door to look out into the darkness. He still couldn't see the owl, although it was certainly there.

"Whhur WoooOOOoooo. Whhurr Wwww Wwww Wwwww wOOOouoooo," it hooted, but this time it sounded slightly further away.

"All right, I'm coming," called Algy, and stepping out of the tree into the night, he jumped into the air.

Once he had left the glowing heart of the tree he found that he was almost blind. There was a faint glimmer of pale light from the stars, which he could see twinkling here and there between the branches above him, but it was not enough light to fly by. "Please wait for me," he shouted, peering anxiously into the night. "I can't see!"

"OOOOoooooooo Whhur Wwww Wwww Wwwww wwWOOOOOOOOOOOooooooooouuu," hooted the owl, and it sounded even more distant than before.

Terrified that he would lose his chance to find the lichens, Algy tried to fly through the trees in the darkness, but he kept bumping into invisible branches.

"Please wait for me!" he called again frantically, as he clung on to a rough bough trying to catch his breath. "I can't keep up in the dark."

"Whhur WoooOOOoooo. Whhurr Wwww Wwww Wwwww wOOOouoooo," the owl hooted once more, but it sounded further away than ever.

Algy took off again and tried to head in the direction of the hooting sound, crashing into branches right, left and centre as he flew wildly through the trees. But before long he noticed that the bumps were getting less frequent. The spaces between the trees were growing larger, and he seemed to be emerging into a clearer area with a little more light. He looked up, and saw a group of what looked like skeleton trees, high on a hillside ahead of him. It was an eerie sight: several stark, dead trees, stripped of their bark, shimmering pale and white in the starlight as though they were ghosts standing silently among the living trees, which merged like shadows into the darkness.

As Algy stared at the ghostly trees he saw the black silhouette of an owl flitting across them, and again he heard a distant "Whhurr Wwww Wwww Wwwww wOOOouoooooo".

"Please wait!" he shouted desperately to the owl, and started flying as fast as he could towards the skeleton trees. Suddenly, he felt an awful bump on his head and fell to the ground, stunned.

For a while Algy just lay there on his back, only half conscious. He listened for the owl's call but he could no longer hear it, and his head felt painful and giddy. Tiny sparkling lights seemed to be spinning around him, and when he tried to sit up, he collapsed in a heap.

Algy waited for a while, and tried again. This time he managed to prop himself up against the tree trunk which had hit him. The lights spinning in his head were gradually slowing down, but he still felt faint and weak, and utterly miserable. Although he had found the Tree with a Golden Heart, he had failed in his mission after all. He had no chance of finding the lichens on his own, and the guide seemed to have vanished into the night.

But as Algy leaned against the knobbly trunk, still half stunned, another part of the rhyme young Flòraidh had taught him began to go round and round in his dizzy head, repeating over and over again:

"If at first you go astray,
  A false guide may have led the way;
  But do not falter, try once more:
  Go back inside that golden door."

Algy tried to concentrate. "Go back inside that golden door!" Of course! That's what he must do! The night was not over yet. Perhaps the owl was not the true guide after all. Maybe he could have another chance...

He pulled himself together and slowly stood up, leaning on the tree trunk for support. Rubbing his bruised head he looked around this way and that, but it was too dark to see beyond the shadowy tangle of branches above him and the vague outlines of one or two other trees nearby, which were just visible against the deep blue night sky. He could still see the eerie skeleton trees gleaming on another hillside not far away though, so it was obvious that he had emerged from the dense part of the wood where the Tree with a Golden Heart grew and was now out in the open somewhere. He would have to go back, but which way was back?

Then, somewhere in the distance below him, Algy caught a glimpse of the tiniest hint of a faint golden glow. Getting to his feet excitedly, Algy forgot about his bruised head and hopped into the air, but immediately dropped back down to the ground. He was still feeling much too wobbly to fly. He would have to walk.

Feeling about on either side for tree trunks, bushes and rocks, Algy started to make his way back down the hill. It was not too difficult to cross the open hillside with the faint gleam of starlight to help him, so he soon found that he was shuffling through the deep carpet of dry leaves which covered the woodland floor, touching one tree trunk after another as he reached out sideways in the darkness of the woods. He hoped fervently that there were no fierce animals about, because the rustling noises he made with every step seemed deafeningly loud to him, and any predator would be sure to hear him coming from a long way off.

Keeping his ears wide open to listen for danger, Algy groped his way around large, moss-covered rocks and rough, gnarled tree trunks, tripping blindly over small stones, ferns, and other plants which grew beneath the trees. He only occasionally caught a glimpse of the golden glow, but it was enough to convince him that he was going the right way.

After stumbling downhill through the trees for some time, he paused to listen, without the distracting sound of his own noisy footsteps. There was a trickle-trickle-trickling sound nearby: the trickling of the hidden burn! He must be almost there, and he guessed that a good part of the night could still lie ahead, as it was absolutely black in the wood. Algy started to feel much happier. Perhaps he really would get that second chance...

Feeling his way carefully around the corner of an enormous rock, Algy stopped. There was the Tree with a Golden Heart, just a short distance away in front of him. The strange, glowing light was streaming out of the heart of the tree into the darkness, and he could see the straggly heather bush leaning across the entrance. He stepped forward eagerly, but as he moved towards the tree he noticed something else. There was a pair of glowing red eyes shining in the blackness, close beside the tree, and they were looking straight at him. He couldn't see the creature they belonged to, but the eyes were keeping absolutely still, very low to the ground.

Algy froze to the spot. Suddenly, the flaming eyes hurtled towards him at incredible speed. Algy panicked and leaped into the air. He crashed his way frantically up through the nearest tree in the darkness, half flying and half climbing, colliding with branches on every side. He rose higher and higher as fast as he could, bumping and bashing, giving no thought to his dazed head or battered body, and then he glanced back down. The eyes were following him up the tree! They were moving rapidly up through the branches, and he thought he could just see the dark shape of a long animal with a bushy tail, climbing and jumping up the tree towards him with great agility.

Algy took only a split second to think. It was an animal. It could climb and leap, and it could surely run... but animals couldn't fly! There was only one thing to do. Algy launched himself into the air and shot upwards into the night, scattering leaves and broken twigs in all directions as he made his way out of the uppermost branches, leaving the fierce red eyes staring angrily up at him from below.

Feeling sick and dizzy from the fright and the effort of flying with a badly bruised head, Algy circled around shakily in the darkness, trying to keep more or less in the same place, and wondered what to do next. He knew that he was safe in the air, but he had to get back to the Tree with a Golden Heart before the end of the night, and that terrible beast was waiting for him. He could still see a glimpse of the golden light below, but how could he return to it without being eaten up before he got there?

Descending cautiously towards the woodland, Algy tried to see whether the fearsome red-eyed animal was still in the top of the tree, but he couldn't be sure. He could no longer see the burning eyes, but that didn't mean the creature wasn't lurking there somewhere, waiting for him to come down again. He tried to think of a way to fool it, but realized that if it remained close to the Tree with a Golden Heart, there was no way he could return without the beast seeing him. Somehow he felt sure that if he could just creep inside the glowing heart of the tree again he would be safe. But getting there was the problem!

Then Algy had an idea. If he could identify the top of the Tree with a Golden Heart and fly into its upper branches, perhaps he could drop very quickly and quietly down, and then sweep into the glowing heart of the tree before the animal had a chance to notice that he had returned. That was the way to do it!

Shuddering with fright, Algy fluttered down slowly, trying to spot the crown of the Tree with a Golden Heart. It wasn't easy, because branches from many different trees criss-crossed each other in the woodland canopy and it was difficult to tell which branch belonged to which tree, especially in the dark. As he got closer to the treetops he could see the golden glow, a little way off to one side, so he moved over and hovered above it. He thought for a moment that he could see the red eyes too, high up in a different tree. Perhaps the creature had not yet returned to the ground. That was lucky! If he acted quickly, he might have a chance...

Algy took a deep breath and dropped into the tree, trying not to think about the fierce animal lying in wait for him. He fluttered down through the branches as fast as he could, until he reached a low branch which stuck out over the woodland floor. Leaping sideways into the air he swivelled round and shot straight into the golden heart of the tree, knocking the heather bush aside as he flew. He didn't look back until he was safely inside the tree, and then, very nervously, he turned and peeped out through the heather door. There were the eyes, glowing fiercely red in the light from the tree, almost no distance away at all... but they didn't move. Algy backed away towards one of the tree's two trunks, and hugged himself tightly against it, hoping and hoping that the creature could not enter the tree. For a while the eyes just remained motionless, staring at him, and then, very slowly, the creature turned away and the eyes were gone. All Algy could see outside the tree was blackness again. The tree had saved him!

Algy collapsed onto the bed of dried leaves which he had slept on earlier in the night, and covered his head with his wings, trying to relax in the warm golden light once again. He was still quivering with fear, but he knew there was no time to lose if he was to have any chance of finding the crottles before the night ended.

"I'm sorry," he whispered to the tree. "I was very stupid. I followed a false guide and got myself into terrible trouble. I'm so sorry to be such a nuisance, but could I please try again? I want so much to find the right medicine for poor Plog."

There was no reply, of course, and Algy did not know what more he could do. He felt dreadfully tired and shaken, and his head hurt. Curling up, he rested his sore head on the pillow of dry leaves. Very soon his eyelids started to feel heavier and heavier, and his mind grew drowsier and drowsier, until – before he knew it – he had fallen fast asleep.

CLICK, CLICK, CLICK, CLICK, CLICK, CLICK, CLICK, CLICK, CLICK, CLICK.

CLICK, CLICK, CLICK, CLICK, CLICK, CLICK, CLICK, CLICK, CLICK, CLICK.

Algy opened his eyes, and for a moment he wondered where he was, but as the golden light washed over him he quickly remembered what had happened. He should not have gone to sleep! Maybe the real guide had come and gone, and he had missed his chance again.

Anxiously, he peeked out through the heather door, and was relieved to see that it was still pitch black out there, and there was no sign of any terrifying red eyes. Perhaps it was not too late after all.

CLICK, CLICK, CLICK, CLICK, CLICK, CLICK, CLICK, CLICK, CLICK, CLICK.

There it was again, the funny little sound that had woken him up. It was just the faintest sort of clickety noise, barely more than a whisper, but with a definite, ticking kind of rhythm to it, and it was coming from somewhere very close by.

CLICK, CLICK, CLICK, CLICK, CLICK, CLICK, CLICK, CLICK, CLICK, CLICK.

CLICK, CLICK, CLICK, CLICK, CLICK, CLICK, CLICK, CLICK, CLICK, CLICK.

It seemed to be behind him now. After his encounter with the fearsome red-eyed beast, Algy was feeling very jumpy, and he swung round quickly in alarm, then backed away towards the heather door.

Just above his head, an extraordinary little brown furry face was staring at him from the underside of the arch formed by the two trunks of the tree. It had bright black eyes, a small round nose, and huge, curved, pointy ears – huge for its minute size, that is, for the tiny creature's face was smaller than Algy's foot. At first Algy couldn't make out what it was. All he could see was the tiny little face, surrounded by the glowing golden light. But it looked far too small to be a threat, and it had a gentle expression, although rather odd.

"Ummm, hello," said Algy, who was not at all sure what to say in such unusual circumstances. "Are you the guide?"

The little creature did not speak, but it opened its tiny mouth once or twice, silently, and Algy caught a glimpse of what looked like remarkably sharp, miniature teeth. It made no move towards him, though, so hoping that it had no intention of biting him, Algy spoke again.

"I've come here to ask for help," he said. "My friend Plog the frog has been terribly ill with the bog fever, and now his mind is damaged. I need to find the right medicine for him, and I was told that if I slept here in the Tree with a Golden Heart, and asked for help, a guide would take me to find the lichens that Plog needs for his crottle porridge."

The little creature looked at him with its bright, black eyes, and then wiggled the curving tips of its enormous ears. Suddenly, it took off, shot out through a gap above the heather bush in the doorway, and started to circle round and round outside the tree, flying very rapidly indeed in a strange, fluttery sort of way.

Algy was astonished. He peered out through the heather door at the flitting creature. Of course! It was a bat! He certainly wasn't afraid of bats.

Algy moved quickly to the heather doorway and looked out. The bat was flying round and round and round the tree, and each time it passed him he could hear that special clickety sound:

Click, click, click, click, click, click, click, click, click, click.

Click, click, click, click, click, click, click, click, click, click.

It seemed to be waiting for him to come out, so Algy stepped warily through the heather door once more, keeping a sharp lookout for the red eyes. But there were no eyes to be seen except the bright black eyes of the bat, which shone with the glowing light from the tree. Algy hopped forward, and the bat immediately started to flit away into the wood.

"Please wait for me," Algy called, taking off into the blackness. But this time it was not entirely dark, for a faint golden glow followed the bat wherever it went, leaving a dim but very pretty trail of light behind it. The bat did not fly in a straight line, but flitted here and there among the trees, round and about and round again, in a bizarre path that made no sense. It would have been impossible to follow if it had not been for the trace of golden light, and even with that aid Algy found it difficult to take the same route as his guide.

Algy's head was still feeling dizzy, and once again he kept bumping into branches, but he managed not to lose sight of the glowing trail that followed the bat, even though he could see no more of the tiny creature itself than an occasional blurry flutter of its rapidly-beating wings.

Confused by the bat's remarkably elaborate path through the dark woods, Algy felt as though he had been flying round and round in circles for ages when finally the golden light stopped moving and came to rest. As Algy flew onwards to catch up with the bat, he saw that it had landed on an exceptionally long, arched branch of a very old tree. The branch curved all the way across in front of him like the bow of a rainbow, and the bat was crouching right in the centre of the arch, wiggling its amazing ears.

The ancient branch was lit up by the golden glow which surrounded the bat, and as he carefully flew in to land beside his tiny guide, Algy could see an extraordinary growth of three different lichens on the bark: one dangled down from the branch like a straggly beard of long grey curly hairs, one grew upwards like a tiny forest of miniature grey-green trees, and one spread out almost flat against the rough bark like a collection of pale flower petals with curled-up edges, all joined together.

## ≈≈ Chapter 8 ≈≈
### The Laird of the Sky

♪ ♪ Tweeetle tweetle tweeeeetie tweetle tweetie tweetie tweetle tweet ♫♫♬♬♫♩♫♩ Good morning, morning, morning on this lovely, lovely day ♫♫♩ And how are you this sunny morning? Tweetle tweetie tweet ♫ ♫♩ It's a gorgeous day for singing, for singing a happy song ♫♪♫♩ Rise and shine, the day is fine ♫♫ ♩ ♫♩ Tweetle tweeeetie tweet ♫♫♪♩♩

The tuneful voice of the robin roused Algy from a deep sleep. He felt extraordinarily tired, and opening his eyes required more effort than he could manage at first. He mumbled drowsily, "Good morning! That's a beautiful song," and then just lay there listening, with his eyes still closed.

Tweeeeetie tweetle ♬ ♬♪ ♫ Sleepy head, up you get and leave your bed ♬♩♩♬♩ sang the robin. You must travel far today, far away you fly today ♫♪♫♩ Tweetie tweetle, far away ♫♩ You must travel far today, tweetie tweetle tweetie tweet ♬♫♫ ♩

Far away? Algy's mind was foggy and confused. He was sure there was something he ought to remember, but he couldn't think what it was. Far away? Where was he? Algy felt about slowly with the tips of his wings. He was lying on a bed of dry leaves as usual, but it didn't feel like his own nest. He tried to sniff the air, and realized with a shock that he had something in his beak – something very peculiar.

Algy sat straight up, with his eyes wide open, and dropped the contents of his beak into his lap. There lay a large bunch of lichens, of three different kinds. One looked like a thin, straggly grey beard, one looked like a tiny forest of miniature greyish-green trees, and one, which was almost flat, looked like a collection of pale flower petals with curled-up edges, all joined together. Algy gazed at them in astonishment.

Gradually, he began to remember the events of the night before: the amazing golden light inside the tree, the frantic flight following an invisible owl through the woods in the darkness and the slow return on foot, then his narrow escape from the creature with the terrifying red eyes. He had just managed to get safely back inside the glowing tree, and then... then everything was hazy.

Algy concentrated hard, grasping at the fleeting images that came and went in his mind. It was exactly like trying to remember a dream that starts to vanish the moment you wake up. Hadn't there been a bat – a strange little bat with a sweet furry face and remarkably large ears? And then some kind of crazy second flight, flitting about this way and that all over the place, following a glowing trail through the wood? But that was all he could remember, and the details were fading fast. He stared at the lichens in his lap once again. He had got them! He had got the crottles for the porridge that would heal his friend Plog!

"Hooray!" cried Algy. "Hooray! Hooray! Hooray! I've got them! Look, I've got them! I've got the lichens!"

*Tweetie tweet, that's good to see ♫ ♪ ♫ ♩ Lichens three from an ancient tree ♫ ♪ ♫ ♩* sang the robin merrily.

Algy could still hardly believe his eyes. Surely it must have been a dream, and yet there were the lichens, sitting in his lap, fresh and real. Without thinking, he reached up and rubbed the top of his head. It felt bruised, as though he had hit it on something very hard. Now he could remember... he had flown headlong into an enormous tree trunk in the night, while trying to catch up with the owl. The pain in his head certainly didn't feel like a dream!

Tweetie tweet ♪♩ It's time to go. Don't be slow, it's time to go ♪♩♪♪♩ Tweetle tweetle tweetie tweet ♫ ♫ ♩ ♩ sang the robin.

"You're absolutely right," said Algy. "Now that I've got the lichens I must get back as soon as I can."

Feeling more alert, Algy looked around. He was still inside the heart of the tree, but there was no sign of any golden glow, except for the morning sun, which was streaming through the woodland canopy, making all the leaves shimmer green and gold. The woods looked very pretty and inviting, but entirely normal. There was really nothing odd about the scene at all, except for the unusual shape of the cloven tree.

Algy reached out to either side and stroked the rough bark of the double tree trunk with his feathery wing tips. "Thank you, kind Tree with a Golden Heart," he whispered softly. "Thank you very much indeed!"

Then, gathering up the lichens in his beak, Algy brushed back the heather in the doorway as gently as he could and eased himself out of the tree. Even in the daytime it seemed to be much colder outside the tree than within its heart, and he felt strangely reluctant to leave, but he knew that he must. His friends would be waiting anxiously, and Plog needed his medicine.

Placing the lichens carefully on a soft cushion of moss, Algy looked up at the robin. "Thank you for all your help," he said. "I could never have found the Tree with a Golden Heart without you, and if I hadn't found the tree, I'd have no cure for my friend. I'm going to make a song about how you helped me, and one day I will come back and sing it for you."

Singing, singing, sing all day ♩♫ ♫♩ Tweetie tweet, singing's sweet ♫♩ sang the robin.

"I wish I could stay and sing with you now," said Algy, "but I really have to go. I need to find my way back home, and that may take some time."

Tweetie tweetle tweetie tweet ♩ ♫ ♩ ♩ Through the trees then fly up high ♫♩♫♪♩ Fly up high, up to the sky, tweetie tweetle, fly up high ♫ ♩ sang the robin.

"Do you mean I should go up the hill through the wood, and not down towards the loch?" asked Algy.

You'll see much more if you fly up high ♫♫♪♫♪♩ Tweetie tweetle high in the sky ♫ ♩ ♩ ♫♩

"Thank you," said Algy. "I certainly won't forget you!" Bending down, he picked the three lichens up again, then shook his head vigorously to make quite sure that they wouldn't fall while he was flying. Waving cheerfully at the friendly robin, Algy took one final look at the remarkable tree, then started to fly through the woods away from the loch, as the robin had suggested.

Most of the trees he passed at first were ancient oaks, massive and gnarled, with long twisting branches covered in lichens and moss. But as he flew further up the hillside the oaks gave way to slender silver birches, and soon Algy found that he was emerging into the open, just as he had in the night. The hill continued to rise ahead of him, and he flew onwards and upwards, over steep slopes of rough grass and bracken, until he reached a high rocky point. Resting there for a moment, Algy gazed out at the view.

It was a beautiful autumn day, and although a bank of dark cloud was hanging low over the horizon in the distance, the air was clear. The silver loch stretched out as far as he could see in both directions, and looking along the water to the right it was obvious that the first stage of the journey was going to be easy. If he simply followed the shore of the loch, retracing the route he had come with the swans, he could not go wrong.

Gripping the lichens as firmly as he could without damaging them, Algy hopped back into the air. He wondered whether there might be a short cut that would get him home more quickly, but as he flew higher he could see that beyond the hilltops there were other ridges further inland, and yet more bleak crags and high peaks beyond those. It looked like a wild and lonely landscape, and none of it was familiar. Algy decided not to take any chances; he could easily get lost in this strange land, especially if the weather changed and the mist came down. It might mean a longer flight, but it would be much safer to follow the loch.

So, dropping down close to the water, Algy started to fly along the shore of the loch, with the early morning sun behind him. Before very long he came to a wide, curving bay, with a stony beach and a steep, wooded hill on the further side which projected some distance into the loch. Rising up into the sky, he flew over the hilltop and was happy to see that he was above the half moon bay where the swans had landed to forage. The shape of the bay was quite unmistakable, even though he had only seen it vaguely in the mist before.

Algy was delighted to have come so far so quickly. The half moon bay looked very attractive in the sunshine, with its velvety terraces of close-cropped grass rising up the mountainside above the water. It was an ideal place to relax on a warm autumn day, and Algy wondered whether he could spare the time for a short rest. Although the lichens were not heavy, it was difficult to keep a firm grip on them, and his beak and face muscles were beginning to ache. He was afraid that he might drop the precious medicine while he was flying, if he didn't stop to rest from time to time.

Sweeping over the meadow by the beach where the swans had landed, Algy headed for a spot high on the hillside beyond. He could see a thicket of windswept rowan trees and hazel bushes growing there, in a gully beside a tumbling burn, and he had not had anything to eat since the morning of the day before.

He fluttered in among the trees, looking for a safe place to store the lichens while he ate, but could not see anything suitable. Then he noticed that some of the rowan berries had fallen to the ground in small clusters. They must be very ripe! Perhaps he could shake some more of them down and eat them on the grass, keeping the lichens safe beside him.

Algy hopped up onto a rowan branch and started bouncing up and down, shaking the tree as hard as he could. Soon there was a shower of lovely orange-red berries falling all around him. Flying over to a hazel bush he did the same thing, and managed to knock a few nuts down to the ground. Then he dropped back onto the grass, arranged the lichens very carefully by his feet, with his toes resting lightly upon them to hold them in place, and started to enjoy the feast. Delicious!

When he had eaten all the nuts and berries he could reach, Algy leaned back contentedly against the rowan tree and gazed up at the sky. The bank of cloud in the distance seemed to be somewhat larger and darker than before, but the sun was shining all around him and it was still quite early in the day. Plenty of time yet! It wouldn't be sensible to set off so soon after a large meal, so he decided to relax for a little while longer, in order to prepare himself for the more difficult stage of his journey...

Split, splat, plopple-plop, splot, splat, spitter spatter.

Plip, plop, spitter spatter, splot, plop, plipple-plopple.

What? What was that? Algy sat up in alarm. He was soaking wet. It was raining heavily, and the world had turned dark grey. Horrified, he looked down at his feet, but it was all right. The lichens were still there. Covering them rapidly with his wings, Algy scolded himself. "You stupid fluffy bird!" he exclaimed out loud. "What an idiot! How could you make the same mistake twice? Stupid, stupid bird!"

He looked up at the sky, and then out across the bay, as far as he could see. There was no way of knowing how long he had slept but it must have been quite some time, because there was nothing out there now except huge black clouds and a great deal of rain.

Algy wondered what chance he had of finding his way home in those conditions, but unless he was prepared to wait until the next day there was nothing he could do but try. So, tucking the lichens as far inside his beak as possible, to protect them from the weather, he flew up into the wet, grey sky, high above the half moon bay. He could not see far in the heavy rain, but he thought that he could spot the gap between the hills which he had flown through with the swans.

Algy headed quickly for the gap, and was relieved to find that it did indeed lead to the bowl-shaped area of moorland he remembered. Battling onward through the drenching rain he crossed the middle of the bowl, with the ground beneath him rising steadily towards a high pass. He felt sure that the long dark loch lay beyond that pass, and as he struggled on, with water pouring off his back and wings, he saw the dark loch, looking blurry and grey at the bottom of a deep valley.

Remembering that the swans had flown high above the loch, level with the forest near the top of the hillside, Algy tried to do the same. But the wind was growing wilder and the rain was driving horizontally against him, and despite his efforts to shelter the lichens they were getting battered and soaked, and so was he.

It was no good; even if he could survive the assaults of the weather the lichens could not. He would have to take cover and wait for the storm to pass.

Luckily, the edge of the great forest was close beside him. Algy turned, and tried to fly in among the trees. But they were mainly evergreen pines and spruces, growing very close together, with many sharp needles that stuck out in every direction, and he could not make his way through the dense, spiky branches. Just as he had decided that he would have to land, he felt a horrible bump on the head again and fell tumbling down, reaching the forest floor much faster than he had intended.

"Ouch!" he cried as he hit the mossy ground, and he reached up with his wing to rub his sore head. Trees always seemed to hit him in the same spot, and there was a nasty lump there now. Massaging his head gently, Algy looked around, and was surprised to see a little face staring at him from among the tangled roots of a huge upturned tree, which must have fallen during a previous storm.

"Hello," said Algy.

"Hello," squeaked the little mouse. "Who are you?"

"I'm Algy," said Algy. "I'm trying to find my way home. I came into the forest to take cover from the storm, but I flew into a tree."

The little mouse giggled. "Oh, I'm sorry," it squeaked. "It's no' funny really, but are you not supposed to be able to fly without hitting the trees?"

"Well, I don't seem to be very good at it any more!" said Algy, rubbing his head again. "But I'm not really used to flying through forests. I live in the Bay of the Sand Islands. Do you know where that is?"

"Aye, aye," squeaked the mouse. "In a way I do, and in a way I don't."

"What do you mean?" asked Algy.

"I've loads of cousins in the Bay o' the Sand Islands," squeaked the mouse, "but I've no' been there myself. It's too far for a wee one like me."

"Is it far for a bird to fly?" asked Algy.

"I dinna ken," squeaked the mouse, and it giggled again. "I'm no' a bird."

"Is Wee Katie MacDougall one of your cousins?" asked Algy. "She's a good friend of mine."

"Is that so!" squeaked the mouse. "Aye, she would be my cousin all right. She'd be a wee bit far removed maybe, but we're all MacDougalls hereabouts."

"Well, I wonder whether you could help me," said Algy. "I'm trying to find my way back home, but I don't know which way to go from here. Can you tell me which direction to take?"

"I've no' been to the Bay o' the Sand Islands myself, like I was saying," squeaked the little mouse again, "but I can maybe point you in the right direction, if you'll come through the forest to the other side."

"Are you sure you know the way?" said Algy. "I don't want to go wrong, because I've got to get back to my sick friend in a hurry."

"Aye, I can tell you how to set off all right," squeaked the mouse, "but you'll maybe need to ask again in a wee while. I'm sorry your friend's no' well!"

The tiny creature leaped off the roots of the fallen tree and started running across the forest floor.

"Please wait for me!" Algy cried. "I'm much bigger than you. I can't move through the trees as fast as that!"

He picked up the lichens, which had dropped from his beak when he fell, and hurried after the little mouse. But the floor of the forest was covered in an exceedingly wet, deep, soggy carpet of mosses and old pine needles, with waterlogged ground beneath, and Algy's feet sank down into it with every step. He tried to fly, or at least to flutter close to the ground, so that he could see the mouse, but there were so many tree trunks, both standing and lying all higgledy-piggledy where they had been knocked down by the storms, that he could only proceed very slowly.

"Wait for me!" Algy called again, but the little mouse scurried away, and Algy just had to follow it as best he could, stumbling over logs and bumping and scratching himself again at every twist and turn.

Eventually, after what seemed to Algy like a dreadfully long and uncomfortable trek, he glimpsed patches of grey daylight beyond the trunks of the trees ahead. Pressing on more eagerly, he finally caught up with the mouse, who was sitting on a cushion of moss beneath one of the tall pines at the forest's edge, washing its ears.

"See the hill there," squeaked the mouse, pointing out beyond the trees with one of its tiny hands.

Algy gazed at the scene in front of him. There was a wide expanse of bleak moorland beyond the forest, with a long, high ridge behind it. He didn't recognize the area, but it was possible that it was one of the places he had flown over with the swans in the mist.

"You'll need to cross that hill," squeaked the mouse. "The Bay o' the Sand Islands is away over there, but I canna tell how far."

"Are you quite sure?" asked Algy.

"Aye, aye. There's a wee black and white bird that passes by here from the Bay, when the summer comes to an end. That's the way he comes, right enough. And he gocs back the same way in the spring. Always the same. 'Just a dip and a bob,' he says."

"Thank you!" said Algy. "That's a big help. I know that black and white bird! You've been very kind."

"I hope you make it home," squeaked the little mouse. "And I hope your friend gets well. Remember me to all the wee folk in the Bay. Tell them Wee Angus from the great forest was asking for them."

"I'll do that," said Algy. "And thank you again." He looked out across the moor. The rain had almost stopped, but the wind was as strong as before, if not stronger. He could see the brown grasses waving and bending right down to the ground, and bits of twigs and leaves flying about all over the place. Algy wondered whether he should stay in the forest for a while longer, but there was no sign that the weather would change, and he was afraid the lichens would not stay fresh.

"I'd better be going," he called to the little mouse. "Goodbye!" He leaped into the air and started to fly across the open moor. The wind was blowing crossways to the direction he was heading, so it was almost impossible to fly straight, but he battled against it until he managed to reach the long ridge. Struggling up to a high point, Algy paused for a moment, sheltering the lichens with his wings.

Looking round to his right he could see a glimpse of the ocean, but the islands were hidden by the low clouds and he didn't recognize the coastline. Away on his left he could also see the gleam of water, which he guessed must be the silver loch. But he couldn't see the Bay of the Sand Islands anywhere, and had no idea where it might fit in to the coastline. The mouse had said that it lay beyond the ridge, but there were many more rocky ridges on the far side of this one, and he had no idea which direction to take.

Although the clouds were not as dense as before, the light was growing dimmer, and Algy feared that it must be almost evening. He would have to press on quickly, as he dared not spend the night out in the open on the top of some exposed peak.

Jumping back into the air, Algy headed for the next line of crags. But the wind at that height was gusty and strong, and Algy was aware that he was being swept sideways, along the top of a narrow ridge with bare, rocky points sticking out at all angles. He decided that he would have to land and take cover again, before he was blown off course completely. Looking down, he spotted a small rainwater pool in a scoop in the rock, high up on the ridge among the crags. There were a few clumps of brown grass growing beside the pool, and it was sheltered by a tall cliff of bare rock.

Algy dropped down through the air, fighting against the wind, and managed to land on the rough grass beside the pool. He quickly backed up close to the rock for maximum protection from the weather, and leaned against the stone wall wearily. He felt exceedingly tired: it was hard work flying through the wind and the rain, especially after an exhausting night. But it was much calmer in the shelter of the crag, so he placed the lichens carefully under one foot and tried to rest a little before pressing on again.

All of a sudden, Algy became aware of a presence in the sky. He wasn't looking in that direction, but somehow he could tell that there was something terrible up there, and he didn't want to know what it was. A moment later, a huge dark shape plunged down towards him at terrific speed. Algy shot straight up into the air without a second's thought, forgetting all about the lichens in his fright. The enormous bird swooped round and started to pursue him, and as Algy desperately tried to escape, Ruaridh's words came back to him. "If you should see him, fly way up high. You'll be safer there. And if there is nothing else you can do, attack!"

Algy looked back at the gigantic bird following him. Attacking something so massive and fierce was completely out of the question! Panic-stricken, he tried to climb higher, struggling against the fierce wind and yelling "Help! Help! Help! Help! Help!" at the top of his voice. He knew it was crazy. Who could even hear him, high over those crags in stormy weather, never mind help him? But even the slightest chance was better than none, so he kept on crying "Help! Help! Help! Help! Help!" while he ascended higher and higher into the sky. He had never flown so fast before, but he feared that the eagle was gaining on him all the same.

Just as his strength was about to fail, and he was almost at the point of despair, Algy thought he heard a familiar sound. Could that really be a voice, or was it the roaring of the wind around his wings? He tried to listen while he dodged wearily from side to side in a final, frantic attempt to throw off the eagle.

"Cawwwwwwww, cawwwwwwww, cawwwwwwww! Cawwwwwwww, cawwwwwwww, cawwwwwwwwww!"

Algy couldn't believe it. It sounded exactly like the hooded crows, but surely that was impossible.

He swooped round in a circle and looked in the direction the sound seemed to be coming from.

"Cawwwwwwww, cawwwwwwww, cawwwwwwww! Cawwwwwwww, cawwwwwwww, cawwwwwwwwww!"

It was the crows! Two large hooded crows were flying rapidly towards him, their black wings beating fast and hard as they approached. "No worries, Algy!"

one of them cawed loudly as it swept past him and flew straight at the eagle, who had almost caught him. To Algy's astonishment the eagle did not attack, although the crow was a very much smaller bird, but just hung there hovering in the air.

"Down you go, Algy," cawed the second crow, as it too flew straight towards the eagle. Although he wanted to help the brave crows, Algy was so exhausted that he simply couldn't manage to remain in the sky a moment longer. There was nothing he could do but drop back down to the ridge as the crow had instructed, and wait to see what happened.

Landing in the first spot he could find, Algy crouched trembling beneath a crag and gazed upwards, terrified that the eagle would attack his friends. But he was amazed to see that it was the other way round. The eagle dropped a little way in the air and the two crows pursued him, circling over the enormous bird and taking turns to dive at him with their beaks extended.

The eagle soared this way and that, trying to shake off the hooded crows, but although they did not leave him alone for a moment, the mighty bird of prey made no attempt to fight back. Before very long, he simply seemed to get bored with their attentions. Turning his back on the attackers, the great eagle swooped round in the air with his huge, jagged wings outstretched, and swept off majestically into the distance. Algy collapsed in a heap on the ground. He had never been so frightened in all his life, and he was quivering and quaking from top to toe, both from fear and from the physical effort of trying to escape.

As soon as the eagle had gone, the two crows quickly dropped down to join Algy, crying "Cawwwwwwww, cawwwwwwww, cawwwwwwwwwwwwwww!" in triumph.

"Thank you!" Algy stuttered. "Thank you, thank you, thank you! I can't imagine what would have happened if you hadn't turned up just then!" Algy shuddered. He just couldn't stop shaking.

"Nae bother," cawed one of the crows merrily, winking at Algy. It did not seem in the least perturbed by its recent battle with the eagle. "But the Laird o' the Sky's no' one for you to be messing with!"

"Glad we found you," cawed the second crow cheerfully. "We've been out searching for you all day."

"Searching for me!" exclaimed Algy.

"Aye," cawed the first crow. "Searching for you, you daft bird!"

"Oh, I'm so sorry to be such a nuisance," Algy started to say, and then suddenly remembered the lichens. "Oh no!" he wailed desperately. "I've lost the lichens! The precious lichens that I got from the Tree with a Golden Heart. I've lost them! What'll I do?"

"You found them, then?" cawed the second crow.

"Yes, I found them, but now they're gone!" cried Algy miserably, on the verge of bursting into tears. "I left them behind when the eagle attacked."

"I'm no' very surprised at that!" cawed the second crow cheerfully.

"Nae bother," cawed the first crow again. "We'll find them."

"Go on, Algy," cawed the second crow, as it jumped back into the air. "Follow the ridge back a way."

Algy couldn't believe it would be possible to find something so small among all the crags, which stretched as far as he could see in the dim light, and he hardly had the strength to fly, but he was desperate to find the lichens, and didn't want to let his brave friends down. Their cheerful determination made him feel slightly stronger, so calling out "I'm coming," he lifted slowly up into the air once more. He noticed that the wind seemed to be dropping, but it was also beginning to get dark. There was very little time.

"Take it easy," cawed the first crow.

Algy fluttered gradually higher, and studied the crags beneath him. His mind was muddled by exhaustion and the terror of his encounter with the eagle, but he tried hard to remember what the spot he had landed in looked like. There had been a small pool, high on a crag, beside a tall rock wall...

"The place where I left them had a small pool in the rock," Algy called to the crows. "It was high up among the crags, with a few clumps of grass beside it, and a big wall of rock on one side."

"That's fine," cawed the first crow, and the two crows split up and started to fly round and round above the crags in a methodical way, circling over each point carefully before moving on to the next. Algy attempted

126

to search too, but he found it difficult to see in the low light, and he was too tired and distressed to concentrate, so he just tried to keep up with the crows, waiting to see what they might find.

They had travelled some distance back along the line of the crags when the first crow suddenly cawed "Algy!"

Algy flew quickly over to join the crow, and looked down. There it was: the pool he had landed beside before the eagle attacked. He was sure it was the same one, because he recognized the shape of the big crag towering over the spot where he had sheltered from the wind. Joyfully, he swept down to the ground and alighted on the patch of brown grass at the foot of the tall rock. They were still there! The lichens were still there!

"Aye, aye," cawed the second crow, as it came in to land beside him.

"I can't believe it!" Algy cried gratefully. "You really are amazing!"

"Nae bother!" cawed the first crow again, perching on a rocky ledge beyond the tiny pool, and it winked kindly at Algy. "Nae bother."

"That's you then," cawed the second crow to Algy. "Time fluffy birds were in bed!"

"In bed?" said Algy. "What do you mean? Are we near the Bay of the Sand Islands?"

"Aye, it's just over the way there," cawed the first crow. "Can you make it?"

"Make it home?" cried Algy excitedly, even though he was still trembling from shock. "Of course I can, if you show me the way. I had no idea I was so close. That's wonderful!"

"Night's coming on fast," cawed the second crow, hopping up into the air.

"Aye," cawed the first crow, as it followed its friend. "Time we were away." The two hooded crows circled lazily around the big crag in the wind, cawing cheerily to each other as they passed over Algy's head.

"Wait for me!" cried Algy, and he bent down and picked up the lichens in his beak once again. Taking a long, deep breath to stop himself shaking, he lifted off the ground and fluttered unsteadily upwards to join his brave friends.

Then, with one hooded crow on each side of him, Algy flew slowly over the crags in the last grey light of the day, and back to his home in the Bay of the Sand Islands.

"Cawwwwwwww, cawwwwwwww, cawwwwwwwww!" called the crows triumphantly, as they led the way. "Cawwwwwwww, cawwwwwwww, cawwwwwwww, cawwwwwwwwwwwwwwww!"

## ⤳⊙ Chapter 9 ⊙⤳
### Crottle Porridge

Tucked up safely in his own bed, and completely worn out by his adventures, Algy slept long and deeply, until the morning sun started to flicker through the heart-shaped gap in his ivy curtain and the light danced across his eyes. Sitting up, he immediately reached into his special secret cubbyhole in the rock at the back of his nest.

For a moment he feared that the whole adventure might have been nothing more than a strange dream. He could remember Old Eachann and Ruaridh telling him that he must go home and rest, as he was so tired he might fall sick himself. Perhaps he had been so exhausted that he had just imagined all the extraordinary things that had happened after that.

He felt about carefully in the cubbyhole with the tips of his wings. It wasn't a dream! There were the lichens, just as he remembered them. And his head had a nasty lump on it, and his body felt battered and bruised. It must all have really happened after all!

Algy turned round and peeped out through the ivy curtain. The sun had just risen above the Grey Crag, and the day looked fine. Reaching back into the cubbyhole again, Algy carefully extracted the three lichens, one by one, and grasped them firmly in his beak. As soon as he was sure that he had got a good grip on all three, he eased himself slowly out through the ivy curtain and set off, straight over the tops of the dunes towards Plog's bog, taking the shortest route possible.

As he flew up from the Blue Burn towards the bog, Algy could see that Old Eachann and several other birds and animals had gathered at the base of the big rock where Mr Voles had picked so many bog myrtle leaves. They were all looking up towards him, and when Algy flew in to join them, the whole crowd started to cheer and shout "Well done, Algy! Well done, Algy! Well done, Algy!"

Algy felt rather embarrassed, and hardly knew which way to look, but as he still had the lichens grasped in his beak his first concern was to find a safe place to put them down. Old Eachann nodded his head towards a bowl-shaped hollow in the big rock, and Algy landed close beside it, very gently placing the lichens inside the natural stone dish.

"Well done, Algy! Well done, Algy!" they all called again as he came in to land.

Ruaridh the rabbit immediately bounced up to Algy and gave him a big rabbit hug, and Mr Voles dashed up and rubbed his furry face vigorously against Algy's foot, murmuring "Well done, well done, well done," while the other creatures crowded round, patting Algy on the back or applauding with their wings or feet.

"Well done!" Ruaridh snuffled again, twitching his whiskers rapidly. "It's good to see you're safe and sound."

"Safe and sound!" echoed Mr Voles happily. "Safe and sound! Safe and sound!"

"It's very good to be back!" exclaimed Algy, when the commotion had subsided a little and he had managed to catch his breath. "But where's Plog? How is he? Is he all right?"

"He's as right as he was when you left," snuffled Ruaridh, "but no righter."

"I must go and see him," said Algy. "I worried all the time that something would happen to him while I was away and the whole trip would be in vain."

Old Eachann stepped forward. "Algy," he crackled, "we are delighted that you have returned to us without harm. We were aware that you had set off safely with the swans, but beyond that we heard nothing until the hooded crows came back last night. We were all very greatly concerned."

"I'm sorry if I worried you," said Algy. "I didn't mean to cause any alarm. But how did you know I had gone with the swans? And how did Silvie know what I was doing, and where I was going? I've been puzzling over that ever since I set off."

Algy turned towards Ruaridh. "Did you tell somebody what I was doing after all?"

"No," sniffed Ruaridh, twitching his long whiskers. "I didn't say a word." He laughed a snuffly laugh. "I didn't need to! The crows were close by all the time, listening to what we said. You didn't see them in the mist. As soon as you were away, they flew straight up to Old Eachann. He told them to watch the land, and Silvie to watch the sea. Everyone was worried about you."

"You mean everyone knew all the time!" said Algy, feeling rather foolish.

"Aye," snuffled Ruaridh. "That's about it. Silvie came back to say you were away with the swans. But we didn't hear anything after that."

"And you succeeded," crackled Old Eachann. "That is marvellous indeed. In time you can tell us the full story of your adventures, which must surely have been remarkable. It will make a fine tale for a winter's night. But for now we should concentrate on helping Plog."

"I really must go and see him," said Algy. "I've been so worried about him."

"Plog will be happy to see you," crackled the heron. "He is still not able to express himself clearly, but he was alarmed by your absence. You can tell him that we will shortly be bringing him some medicine."

Algy would have liked to watch them prepare the crottle porridge, but he couldn't bear to wait any longer to see Plog, so he flew quickly over to the tussock that he remembered so well... but Plog was not there.

"Plog," he called anxiously. "Plog, where are you? It's Algy. I'm back!"

*"Not far away now,*
  *Bird again, back in bog,*
  *All fluffy, fluffy nice in the grass."*

Algy stared towards the spot where he thought the croaking was coming from, but at first he could see no sign of his friend. Then he saw two familiar bulgy eyes looking at him, and there was Plog, half immersed in the water once more, with a big grin on his face.

"Hello Plog," said Algy happily, as he found himself a perch near the edge of the bog pool. "I see you're feeling better. That's wonderful!"

*"Gurgly-gurgle with the fishes,*
  *Every wet and suchlike swimmy;*
  *Legs wobbly-bendy, here and there,"*

croaked Plog.

"I'm so glad," said Algy encouragingly. "You look much better than when I saw you last. But soon you'll feel even better still. I found the medicine for you!"

*"Nasty yuchhhhhhhh?"* croaked Plog.

"I suppose it may taste rather nasty, yes," said Algy. "But I'm afraid you must take it all the same. They are just preparing some now." He pointed towards the big rock, and saw that Old Eachann was stalking slowly and squelchily across the bog towards them. Without a word the old heron walked right up to Plog, picked him up gently in his beak, and deposited him back in the middle of the grassy tussock where he had lain sick for so long.

*"Urghhhhhhhhhhhhhhhh!"* croaked Plog in protest, but he did not attempt to move away once Old Eachann had put him down.

"Now Plog," crackled the heron, "Algy has undertaken a difficult and dangerous mission to find this medicine, at great risk to himself, and I am sure that you will want to take full advantage of his kindness and his bravery. The crows will bring you one small shellful of the crottle porridge three times a day, and you should eat it all up."

As he spoke, one of the hooded crows flew over from the rock, carrying a shallow white shell very similar to the one which had contained Plog's fresh water when he lay ill in bed. With its usual skill, the crow balanced steadily on one leg and tipped its head slowly down into the middle of Plog's tussock while holding the shell level with its other foot. It placed the white shell carefully beside Plog and straightened up again, winking at Algy.

Plog stared at the soggy grey mess which the shell contained. *"Yuchhhhhhhhhhh, yuchhhhhh, yuchhhhhhh,"* he croaked again.

"You really must eat it Plog," said Algy. "Please!"

Plog looked up at Algy and blinked. For a moment he did nothing, then he lifted one of his front legs and carefully covered his nostrils with his long, tapering fingers. Very slowly, he opened his large mouth, leaned towards the shell, and took a deep gulp. When he sat back again, the crottle porridge was gone.

"That's right!" said Algy. "It will do you good, really it will. Though you're supposed to sip it."

*"Nasty yuchhhhhhhhhhhhhhhhhh,"* croaked Plog again grumpily.

"Frog's no' a very good patient," cawed the crow, laughing, and it quickly picked up the empty shell and flew off, cawing merrily.

"The crows will bring the crottle porridge three times a day," crackled Old Eachann again. "Early in the morning, in the middle of the day, and shortly before nightfall."

"And be sure you eat it all up every time!" Algy said firmly.

Plog grimaced, and slowly made his way back towards the pool, half hopping across the bog plants in a wobbly sort of way and half waddling like a toad.

Algy was delighted to see his friend up and about again, but Plog was obviously finding it difficult to move around. Algy turned to Old Eachann. "Do you think the crottle porridge will help strengthen Plog's body as well as his mind?" he asked.

"I have no experience of these crottles," crackled the heron quietly. "I hope that it will, of course, but only time will tell."

Ruaridh bounced over to join them. "How did you like that?" he snuffled at Plog mischievously.

*"Nasty, nasty, nasty yuchhhhhhhhhhhh,"* croaked Plog grumpily from the edge of the water.

"See the thanks you get!" Ruaridh snuffled at Algy. "You'll be wondering why you bothered!"

"Poor Plog," said Algy. "First that awful fever, and now this nasty medicine!"

"Aye, but it will make a new frog of him," snuffled Ruaridh, twitching his whiskers. "You wait and see!"

Plog croaked something under his breath, but fortunately no one could quite hear what he said.

"How did you prepare the porridge?" Algy asked Ruaridh.

"In equal measures, one by one,
  Mashed in water till they're done;
  Add two leaves of meadowsweet,
  Then pound with stick or tread with feet."

"You pounded it?" said Algy.

"We stomped it," snuffled Ruaridh. "Actually, I stomped it, and the other folk just sat about watching."

Algy laughed. "Perhaps I can stomp it with you, next time," he said. "My feet are quite large too!"

"Perhaps you can stomp it instead of me, next time," snuffled Ruaridh, twitching his whiskers again. "Now that's a fine idea."

"But what's meadowsweet?" asked Algy. "I don't know what that is."

"Have you not seen the meadowsweet growing about the place? There's a grand patch right in your own garden, to be sure," snuffled Ruaridh.

"My garden?" said Algy, surprised. "What garden?"

"That wee grassy spot down among the rocks, where all the flowers grow," sniffed Ruaridh. "Close by your nest."

"Oh, I know the place you mean," said Algy. "It's a pretty spot, certainly. I often perch on a rock there and watch the sea."

"Aye, and there's plenty meadowsweet down by the wee burn there," snuffled Ruaridh. "You could maybe bring us some. It's no' easy to find it here."

"That's right," crackled Old Eachann. "It would help if you could bring the meadowsweet leaves, Algy. And I do not think it would be wise to leave the lichens exposed on the rock here. We have no safe storage place close by the bog. If you were to keep the crottles in the darkness at the back of your nest in the cliff, they would remain in good condition."

"Do you mean that I should bring the lichens and the meadowsweet three times a day?" Algy asked.

"Does the crottle porridge have to be made fresh every time?"

"It would be foolish not to make a fresh mixture for each dose," crackled Old Eachann. "The porridge will not keep well, once it has been pounded. Wait for me on the rock, and I will show you what portion of the crottles to bring. Ruaridh can hop across the dunes and point out the meadowsweet which grows by your nest. We will only need a few leaves at a time."

"All right," said Algy, "I'll be happy to do that, if you think it's the best way."

Waving a wing at Plog, who seemed to be dozing among the sodden grasses in the shallow water at the edge of the deep bog pool, Algy flew over to the rock and waited for Old Eachann to join him. In the bright light of day, the lichens did not look like anything much at all: just a small pile of peculiar, dry-looking, straggly greenish-grey and flabby white bits and pieces, lying limply in the hollow in the rock. Algy wondered whether they could really help Plog recover his mind and his sense of rhyme, or whether it was just an old folk tale without any truth to it. But there was only one way to find out, and he supposed that as long as the porridge could do his friend no harm, it was certainly worth a try.

So, from then on, Algy flew backwards and forwards to Plog's bog every morning, noon and early evening, carrying a little bit more of the lichens each time, together with a few fresh meadowsweet leaves.

He helped Ruaridh stomp the lichens into the crottle porridge with his feet, and he always made sure that Plog ate up all his nasty medicine. When it wasn't porridge time, Algy spent most of his days just keeping Plog company, telling him about his remarkable adventure. But although Plog seemed interested, and croaked quite happily at Algy and his other friends, what he said made only a small amount of sense at best, and often made no sense at all.

None of Plog's friends expected to see instant results from the crottle porridge. They all knew that medicines might take some time to work, so when there was no immediate change in Plog's condition, Algy just waited patiently. But as day followed day once more and Plog continued to babble nonsense, Algy began to wonder whether his friend was ever going to recover. Plog did not seem to be unhappy, now that he was able to move around in the water again, and he was growing gradually stronger, but there was very little change in the state of his mind, and he did not recover his sense of rhyme.

Before long, the moon had grown almost round again and still there was no sign of improvement in Plog's mental condition.

On the last night before the moon was completely full, Algy lay awake in his nest, fretting about his friend. The bright white moonlight was flooding through every little gap in his ivy curtain, preventing him from falling asleep, and he tossed fitfully this way and that.

He tried to concentrate on the soothing lullaby of the sea. It was a fine, calm night, and he could hear the waves on the sand very clearly.

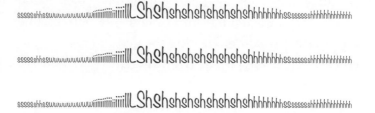

But although the sound was comforting, Algy felt miserable. If only he could do something more to help his friend... but no one knew what more could be done. They had done everything they could, and Plog had not recovered. "Poor Plog," thought Algy sadly, as he dozed on and off. "Poor old Plog!"

By the time the moon sank down into the sea and the sun began to rise, Algy was feeling thoroughly tired and depressed. He had tossed and turned all night in the dazzling moonlight, worrying about Plog. Lying back wearily on his bed of dried birch leaves and heather flowers, he wondered what the new day would bring. There were just a few tiny scraps of lichen left in his cubbyhole – about enough for one final shellful of crottle porridge – and it seemed unlikely that a single dose could make any difference at this stage.

Holding his ivy curtain back to the side with one wing, Algy gazed out at the early morning sunshine. It was a beautiful autumn morning, with the sea beginning to sparkle and dance against a deep blue sky and the waves breaking merrily on the beach. If only Plog were well again, it would be a truly lovely day.

Algy sighed and rolled over towards the cubbyhole at the back of his nest. As he reached into the secret hiding place for the last pieces of lichen, he heard a mouse's voice calling to him from below.

"Algy, Algy, Algy, Algy!" it squeaked excitedly.

Algy turned back towards his door, pushed aside the curtain, and called "Who's that down there?"

"It's Wee Katie," squeaked the little voice. "Will you come down? I've news!"

Somewhat reluctantly, Algy eased himself through the ivy curtain and dropped down the cliffside to perch on a ledge where lush green ferns and a wild rose grew in a pocket in the rock. Looking down at the ground, he could see Wee Katie sitting on a mossy stone, with her front legs stretched up against the cliff as she peered upwards towards him.

"Hello Katie," said Algy. "What's happened now?"

"You'll no' believe it!" squeaked the voice.

"Won't believe what?" asked Algy anxiously. "What's happened? Is Plog worse?"

"He's no' worse, he's better!" squeaked the little mouse, jumping up and down on the moss. "The Bard has got the rhymes again! As soon as he woke up this morning, he sent for you... in rhyme! They say he's quite himself again!"

"Really?" exclaimed Algy in great excitement. "Are you sure?"

"Aye, aye," squeaked Wee Katie. "The Bard croaked this rhyme:

"Quick, quick, fetch Algy, bring him here!
For all at once my mind is clear.
Go swiftly to his cliffside nest
And rouse him from his well-earned rest:
Say he and I must make some rhymes,
Just like we did in former times;
And I must thank him, and then soon
We'll sing and dance beneath the moon!"

"I remembered it all," squeaked Wee Katie proudly. "It was Ruaridh's wee niece Flòraidh who came to tell me. She's a one for the rhymes!"

"That's amazing!" cried Algy. "I can hardly believe it! I'll go over there at once. Do you think I should take the last bits of lichen? I was just about to get them."

"I dinna ken," squeaked Wee Katie. "I've not had any word about that."

"Well, perhaps I'd better," said Algy. "I think Old Eachann said that they should all be used up. It does seem a pity to waste them."

"Maybe you're right," squeaked the mouse. "But I'll be getting back now. They'll be having a ceilidh, now that the Bard's recovered. I'll need to get ready!"

"A ceilidh?" said Algy. "What's that?"

"A ceilidh. With singing and dancing and suchlike," squeaked Wee Katie.

"Oh, you mean a party!" exclaimed Algy.

"It'll no' be a party. It's a ceilidh," insisted the little mouse. "A ceilidh for the Bard."

"That sounds wonderful," said Algy. "I'll fly over there straight away."

"Will you not need to freshen up a wee bit first?" giggled Wee Katie. "You'll no' be going to the ceilidh like that..."

Algy looked at himself. He had to admit that he was rather grubby and dishevelled; he hadn't been taking the usual care of himself since Plog fell ill. "Ummm, well, I suppose you're right," said Algy. "I'll just have a very quick bath, and then I'll fly over."

"I'll see you in a wee while then," squeaked Wee Katie, and she turned and ran off beneath the bushes.

"Thank you for coming to tell me," Algy called after her. "Thank you very much indeed – that's the best news I've ever heard!"

## ～⚬ Chapter 10 ⚬～
## A Ceilidh for the Bard

A lgy leaped off the ledge below his nest and flew up to the little burn on the hillside to bathe. If there was going to be a celebration he wanted to be as clean and fluffy as possible, so he splashed about vigorously in the cool water, then preened his feathers thoroughly and fluffed himself up in the sunshine.

Pausing only to pick a few leaves from the meadowsweet plants at the foot of the cliff, Algy returned to his nest, collected the last few pieces of lichen from his secret cubbyhole, and gripped them carefully in his beak together with the meadowsweet leaves for one last time.

Then, easing himself back out through his ivy curtain, he flew off along the beaches towards Plog's bog, just as he had done so many times before – but this time it was different!

The oystercatchers foraging on the tideline called out "Queeeeeeek, quick, quick, quick, quick, quick, quick, quick! Queeeeeeek, quick, quick, quick, quick, quick, quick, quick, quick!" just as they had when Plog first fell ill, but this time Algy was happy to be hurrying to see his friend. Plog was better! Algy could still hardly believe it was true, but what an enormous difference it made to the morning! Suddenly the whole world seemed beautiful again, and Algy began to feel as though a huge weight had been lifted off him.

When he reached the bog, Algy landed on the big rock, just as he had done on every other occasion, and placed the meadowsweet leaves and the last scraps of lichen in the rocky bowl. Ruaridh and Mr Voles were already there, waiting for him, and they rushed up to him as he landed. "Is it really true?" Algy gasped, as soon as he had put the lichens and meadowsweet down.

"Aye, the Bard is quite himself again," snuffled Ruaridh, and Algy was sure that the rabbit was smiling behind his whiskers.

"Quite himself again," agreed Mr Voles happily, rubbing against Algy's foot.

"I didn't think the porridge would work," sniffed Ruaridh, "but something has mended him, to be sure. He's rhyming just like he used to." Ruaridh twitched his nose energetically.

"Just like he used to!" echoed Mr Voles.

"I must go and see him," said Algy. "But shall we still prepare the last bit of porridge?"

"Aye, maybe," snuffled Ruaridh. "We'll need to ask Old Eachann. He's checking on Plog just now."

Algy looked over towards the bog pools. He could see the heron's curved back bent low behind a tussock, and then his long neck became visible, straightening up slowly from the ground. Observing that Algy had arrived, Old Eachann stalked slowly across the bog towards him, as he had done so often recently, still lifting each spindly leg carefully in the air before planting his foot down slowly into the squelchy bog again. Algy wondered whether Old Eachann ever hurried, but he guessed not. Even when Plog had been most seriously ill, the old heron had only ever moved in a slow and deliberate fashion.

"Algy," crackled Old Eachann. "The news today is good indeed! It seems that the crottle porridge has been effective after all, and Plog's mind is healed at last. I must admit that I am surprised at the sudden change in his condition, but there is no doubt that today he is better."

"That's just wonderful!" said Algy. "I'm so relieved! I was beginning to think he would never get better, despite the crottles."

"It certainly was concerning," crackled Old Eachann. "But all is well that ends well, and Plog's mind seems to be more or less fully restored. He is still rather weak, but that is not surprising. I am sure that he will regain his fitness in due course. He is already much stronger than he was when the fever left him."

"Shall we prepare the last dose of crottle porridge all the same?" asked Algy. "These are the very last pieces of lichen. Shall we finish them up?"

"I think so, yes," crackled the heron. "It would seem wise and proper to use all of the crottles you were given. One last dose can certainly do no harm, and it may do some further good."

"Will you prepare the porridge while I go and see Plog?" Algy asked Ruaridh. "I really must see him!"

"Do you not think you should stomp the last of the crottles yourself?" snuffled Ruaridh. "It's you who fetched them, after all."

"Ummm, well, yes, maybe," said Algy. "Perhaps I should stomp them with you."

So for one last time, Algy and Ruaridh stomped the lichens and meadowsweet leaves together with a little water, in a dish-shaped hollow in the rock, to make the soggy grey mess that was crottle porridge.

As soon as the porridge was ready, Algy jumped into the air and flew over to the tussock where Old Eachann had been bending down. There was Plog, squatting half in and half out of the shallow water at the edge of the big bog pool, grinning all over his face.

*"And what have we here?*
*A strange bird's coming near!"*

croaked Plog.

"Plog!" exclaimed Algy. "You really are better! I can't tell you how glad I am!"

*"It's a joyful thing to be jolly and glad:*
*It's really much better than feeling sad,"*

croaked Plog, grinning even more.

"That's certainly true," said Algy, smiling at his friend. "And how are you feeling yourself, now?"

*"I feel like a frog at the start of the spring,*
*Who has nothing to do but to hop and to sing."*

Algy laughed. "I'm so happy to hear that!" he said.

*"But Algy, I must thank you,*
*For without your help in time,*
*I would still be talking nonsense*
*And could not make up this rhyme.*
*Your courage and your kindness*
*I can't properly repay,*
*But I'll make up many rhymes for you,*
*Today, and every day!"*

"Awwww, thank you!" said Algy. "I look forward to that. But you really needn't thank me. I'm just so happy that you're well again! And anyway, I had an amazing adventure finding the crottles. I certainly won't forget that in a hurry, and it will make a fine ballad one day!"

*"And I will make a splendid song,*
*About a bird so kind and strong,*
*Who set out on a journey long*
*To save his ailing friend.*

*With many dangers on the way,*
*He never even went astray!*
*And so I'm well again today:*
*A truly happy end!"*

"Well, that wasn't quite the sort of song I meant," said Algy shyly. "And anyway, I did go astray. In fact, I did some very foolish things! But it's very kind of you."

"There will indeed be songs, and there will be dancing and rejoicing and storytelling," crackled Old Eachann, who had stalked up behind Algy and Plog while they were talking. "For it's not every day that a friend who was sick becomes well again. But before the ceilidh can commence, Plog must eat the last of the crottle porridge."

As he spoke, one of the hooded crows flew over from the big rock and placed the familiar white sea shell on a low grassy tussock near the spot where Plog was reclining in the water. The crow winked at Algy, then flew away, cawing loudly.

"*Yuchhhhhhhhhhhhhhhhhhhh,*" croaked Plog, just as he had done when he first had to eat the porridge.

*"It's really most unnecessary,*
 *To eat that nasty stuff,*
 *Because I'm so much better now*
 *And I have had enough!"*

he croaked in protest.

"It is only right that you should finish the crottles which Algy collected at such great risk to himself," crackled Old Eachann.

"Just one last time," said Algy kindly. "There won't be any more after this. The lichens are all used up now. This is the final dose."

*"I suppose I'll have to take it,*
*As you've been so kind to make it,"*

croaked Plog reluctantly.

"So sup the porridge, you daft frog, and let's be starting the ceilidh!" squeaked a cheeky little mouse, who had hopped over to a tussock nearby.

"Where's the ceilidh being held?" asked Algy. "At the Singing Place?"

"No, we will gather at the back of the big beach, near Wee Katie's home," crackled Old Eachann. "There's enough space for everyone there. I am sure that all the folk who helped to look after Plog will wish to attend, and perhaps many more besides."

"Go on, Plog," snuffled Ruaridh, who had bounced over to join them. "Eat your porridge! It's time for the ceilidh!"

Plog groaned, and pulled himself out of the water. He hopped limply across the soggy bog plants to the tussock, placed his long, tapering fingers over his nose once again, opened his big mouth as wide as he could, and gulped. The last of the crottle porridge was gone...

"Hooray!" cried Algy. "The crottles are all gone, and Plog is well again!"

"That's the grandest excuse for a ceilidh I've heard!" snuffled Ruaridh, twitching his nose at Algy. "I'll see you there!"

"How will Plog get to the beach?" asked Algy. "It's much too far for him to hop, especially while he's still weak from the fever."

"I will carry him in my beak," crackled Old Eachann.

*"The heron is a hunting bird,*
  *The frog should treat with caution,"*

croaked Plog grumpily, under his breath.

"Plog!" exclaimed Algy. "You really mustn't go on saying that! Old Eachann has looked after you all the time since you fell ill, and he has organized everyone else too. You mustn't say things like that!"

Plog looked up at the heron and blinked.

*"Forgive me, please, that's my mistake!*
  *Old habits can be hard to break.*
  *I'm truly grateful for your care;*
  *You may convey me through the air."*

So Old Eachann bent down, lifted Plog carefully in his beak, stretched his long neck upwards into the air, and took off. As he flapped slowly away, Algy could see Plog's legs dangling down out of one side of the heron's long beak and his head hanging out of the other.

"Oh, poor Plog!" cried Algy. "I think I'll go with them and see he's all right."

"Don't you worry," snuffled Ruaridh. "The Bard will be fine. There's no other way, unless he could cling on to my back, maybe."

"I'll see you there," said Algy, jumping into the air, and he rushed after Old Eachann and Plog. But the heron flew almost as slowly as he walked, so Algy caught up with him before he had crossed the Blue Burn, and then flew alongside, keeping an eye on Plog all the time.

"We'll be there in a moment!" he called encouragingly to his friend, as Old Eachann flew sedately above the waving, spiky grasses of the Rustling Dunes. Plog just groaned, with his eyes tightly closed.

But even at a heron's pace it only took a short time to fly across the dunes, and Old Eachann soon dropped slowly down to land beside a flat rock which jutted out from the sand cliff at the back of the beach, not far from Wee Katie's home. Bending his long neck down, Old Eachann placed Plog gently on the rock, and then stalked away to one side.

*"Oh my goodness gracious me!*
*It's worse than travelling by sea!"*

croaked Plog in a shaky voice.

"You'll be all right very soon," said Algy soothingly. "Just rest for a moment and take some deep breaths." He made himself comfortable on the rock next to Plog, and looked at the sea. The waves were splashing prettily on the sand, and the surface of the sea was covered in dazzling, dancing sparkles of light. It certainly was a lovely day for a celebration.

"They're here!" rasped a voice from behind, and Roni the raven swept down to perch on the rock beside Algy and Plog. "Come on out, everybody" she called. "They're here!"

Suddenly, creatures of all kinds started emerging from the dunes, flying, fluttering, hopping, running, skipping and jumping down on to the sandy beach in front of the rock. There were mice of all ages, a flock of hooded crows who all looked very much the same, a family of oystercatchers who flew in crying "Queeeeeeek, quick, quick, quick, quick, quick, quick, quick!", several other sea birds of various kinds, and a few inland birds as well.

Ruaridh the rabbit bounced straight down the sand cliff, bobbing from one sandy hollow to another, with his niece young Flòraidh and many other young bunny rabbits following close behind him, laughing at each other as they tumbled and slid down the steep bank on their fluffy tails.

And last but not least, Mr Voles came puffing along the beach from the direction of the Blue Burn, gasping "Ceilidh, ceilidh, ceilidh," as he hurried along.

"That's right," snuffled young Flòraidh to Mr Voles. "It's a ceilidh for Plog, the Bard of the bog!"

"Attention, please!" rasped Roni loudly, tapping her foot on the rock. "Your attention, please!"

As usual, the younger mice could not stop giggling, but this time Roni did not seem to mind.

"We are holding this ceilidh for two reasons," Roni rasped. "To honour Algy, the foolish but brave and surprisingly fluffy bird, who set off into the unknown, in order to find the crottles to heal his friend Plog... and succeeded!"

"Well done, Algy!" squeaked Wee Katie, and all the crowd joined in, shouting "Hooray for Algy!" and "Well done, Algy!" or just "Bravo!"

"And," rasped Roni, looking rather impatiently at the crowd with her bright black eyes, "and... to celebrate the marvellous recovery of Plog the frog, our beloved Bard of the bog, who has conquered the bog fever and returned to good health... and to us."

"Hooray for Plog!" cried Algy enthusiastically. "Hooray for my friend Plog! Hooray for Plog, the Bard of the bog!" And all the other creatures joined in again, some of them shouting "Hooray for Plog!" or "Hooray for the Bard!" and others "Hooray for Algy!" There was a terrific din, and it did not die down for quite some time.

Eventually, Roni raised her jet black wing in the air again. "I am delighted to say that the Bard has already managed to compose a special poem for this occasion," she rasped. "Quiet, everyone, please! The Bard will recite his poem now."

Plog puffed himself up, cleared his throat noisily, and then slowly began to recite in his croaky voice:

*"On either side the peat bog lie*
  *Tall grasses brown, and outcrops high*
  *Of rugged rocks that touch the sky;*
  *And far above, a bird did fly*
  *To find the tree that stands apart;*
  *And with the white swans he did go,*
  *A-soaring where the wild winds blow*
  *Around the woodland there below*
  *And the Tree with a Golden Heart.*

  *Oak trees shake and birches quiver,*
  *Chilly breezes make them shiver,*
  *By the burn that runs for ever*
  *To the loch that shimmers silver*
  *Near the tree that stands apart;*
  *Seven skerries by the shore*
  *Mark the place for evermore*
  *Where Algy found the heather door*
  *To the Tree with a Golden Heart.*

  *Only robin, bright and early,*
  *Always happy, singing merrily,*
  *Helped the fluffy bird so cheerily,*
  *Helped him see that strange tree clearly:*
  *The ancient tree that stands apart.*
  *And by the moon, that bird so weary*
  *Closed his eyes in the woodland airy,*
  *And listening, whispered 'Is this the fairy*
  *Tree with a Golden Heart?'*

155

*The golden light did shimmer free,*
*Just like a shining star you see,*
*Set in the heart of that ancient tree*
*Where the fluffy bird slept cosily*
*In the tree that stands apart.*
*And when a guide appeared by night,*
*He did not flee or take a fright*
*But followed, in the glowing light*
*Of the Tree with a Golden Heart.*

*He left the tree, he left his bed,*
*At first a false guide blindly led*
*Him where the bravest fear to tread,*
*And from the fearsome eyes he fled*
*To the tree that stands apart.*
*But then a true and trusty guide*
*Showed him where the crottles hide*
*'I've found the lichens,' Algy cried*
*In the Tree with a Golden Heart.*

*And then in blue unclouded weather,*
*He pushed aside the straggling heather,*
*Held the lichens all together,*
*Ascended lighter than a feather,*
*And left the tree that stands apart.*
*And through the bright autumnal day*
*He flew, but soon began to stray,*
*He did not know the proper way*
*From the Tree with a Golden Heart.*

*He left the bay, he crossed the moor,*
*He flew where he had flown before,*
*And recognized the loch he saw*
*When with the swans he had to soar*
*To find the tree that stands apart.*
*Then in the forest, dark and wide,*
*He found help from a tiny guide;*
*'Can you direct me home?' he cried,*
*'Home from the Tree with a Golden Heart?'*

*In the stormy west wind straining,*
*When the light was quickly waning,*
*And the clouds were also raining,*
*Flying on without complaining,*
*That fluffy bird who stands apart.*
*Menaced by the eagle high*
*On the Grey Crag, they heard him cry,*
*And hooded crows did quickly fly*
*To the bird with a golden heart.*

*Who is this? And what is here?*
*When I was ill he stayed so near,*
*And then he fetched the lichens rare,*
*And all the creatures raised a cheer*
*For this bird who stands apart.*
*And soon my mind began to mend,*
*With all my heart I now intend*
*To thank my brave and fluffy friend,*
*The bird with a golden heart."*

The moment that Plog had finished reciting, everyone started to cheer and applaud, and there were many more cries of "Bravo, Plog!" and "Well done, Algy!" The young mice jumped up and down and up and down and up and down on the sand, squeaking "Hooray! Hooray! Hooray! Hooray! Hooray! Hooray!" as they leaped in the air, and young Flòraidh and all her friends and relations crowded round Plog snuffling "Bravo! Bravo! Bravo!"

During the recital Mr Voles had crept up onto the rock where Algy and Plog were sitting, and he was now rubbing himself against Algy's leg. Algy looked down at his furry friend, and Mr Voles whispered "Speech, speech, speech."

Algy got to his feet, and raised his wing as Roni had done, to quieten the crowd. "Before the dancing and everything begins, I would like to say just a few words," he said.

"Just a few words," echoed Mr Voles.

"I'm so grateful for all your kindness, and I am truly honoured by my friend Plog's wonderful poem. I can't imagine how he could have composed it so quickly!"

"Hooray!" squeaked the young mice again, giggling.

"But I really couldn't have done anything without the help of so many friends: Silvie, the company of swans, the robin in the woodland, the mysterious guide in the night, Wee Angus MacDougall – who wants all his cousins here to know that he was asking for them – and the incredibly brave hooded crows, who came out to look for me and saved me from the Laird of the Sky. If it wasn't for the crows, I wouldn't be here now... and Plog would never have got his crottle porridge!"

"Hooray for the hoodies!" squeaked the young mice, jumping up and down even more vigorously. "Hooray for the hoodies! Hooray for the hoodies!"

"Nae bother," cawed one of the hooded crows on the beach, and it winked at Algy and then at the little mice.

*"And please thank all those kindly folk*
 *Who gave up so much time*
 *To help a weak and sickly frog*
 *Who could not even rhyme!*
 *It must have been a dreary business*
 *Tending to a frog,*
 *Spending days and nights on end*
 *Just nursing in the bog,"*

croaked Plog.

"Well, it was different," said Algy, hugging his friend gently. "But don't you get sick again!"

"When'll the dancing start?" squeaked a little mouse, hopping up and down on its toes.

"In just a few moments, I think," Algy said kindly to the mouse. "There's only one thing more. Of course it can't hear me, and it's not exactly a creature like the rest of us, but I want to thank the Tree with a Golden Heart. Without that amazing tree, Plog would not be well today, despite all our efforts. Thank you, tree!"

"Hooray for the Tree with a Golden Heart!" squeaked Wee Katie.

"Hooray for the Tree with a Golden Heart!" echoed Mr Voles and many other creatures.

"Yes indeed," rasped Roni. "But I think that will be enough thanks for now. It's time for some music!"

"Music, music, music, music!" squeaked the young mice enthusiastically, leaping up and down again.

"Come along now, all you wee mice," squeaked Wee Katie. "You come on in and help me fetch the refreshments." She ran into one of the tiny holes that led to her home in the Rustling Dunes, and all the young mice followed her. Very soon they started carrying out large quantities of berries and fruits and nuts and all kinds of good things to eat, and set them all out neatly at the foot of the sand cliff.

Meanwhile, Flòraidh and many of the other young bunnies grouped themselves together beside the rock where Algy was sitting with Plog, and began to sing jolly songs in harmony, while a few who were standing at the back kept time by thumping their feet rhythmically on the ground. In no time at all, most of the assembled creatures were dancing on the beach and the ceilidh really began to get under way.

The rabbits bounced up and down enthusiastically, their fluffy white tails bobbing in the air, the mice leaped around all over the place with enormous energy, Old Eachann and Roni did a slow and stately dance together, and many of the birds hopped about happily, here and there and everywhere. But the hooded crows turned out to be the best dancers of all. They pranced and skipped and fluttered and whirled, this way and that, on one leg and two, in a remarkably elaborate pattern, sometimes in groups and sometimes alone, but always in time to the music. Algy was amazed by the varied talents of his extraordinary hooded friends: he had never seen dancing like that before!

At times Algy himself got up and danced a fluffy dance with the other creatures on the sand, and at times he just perched beside Plog and Mr Voles on the rock at the back of the beach, watching the celebrations.

The day wore on, the tide washed in and the tide washed out, and time passed surprisingly quickly. Before very long, the full moon was beginning to rise above the ridge behind them, bathing the beach with a soft, silvery light.

As the moon climbed higher in the sky it made a beautiful bright white path across the sea, and Algy was thrilled to see Silvie the seal's dark head pop up in the moonlit water. She did not join the dancing on the beach, but she swam in close to the shore, and in the pale, silvery moonlight she crooned a strange and lovely song in that soft language which Algy didn't understand, before vanishing beneath the water again.

The moon rose higher still, and then began its slow descent towards the sea, but the ceilidh carried on. Although most of the creatures would normally have been in bed by nightfall, no one showed the slightest inclination to leave the beach on this very special evening, and they continued to dance long into the night in the lovely clear moonlight, throwing soft, swirling moon shadows onto the ground as they twisted and twirled on the pale sand.

"This has been a truly wonderful day!" Algy whispered to Plog, as the full moon sailed high above the ocean.

"A truly wonderful day," agreed Mr Voles, who was snuggled up against Algy's leg, half asleep.

*"The creatures sang their fanciful songs*
*As they merrily danced and twirled,*
*But I'm happier just to be sitting beside*
*The fluffiest friend in the world,"*

croaked Plog sleepily. Algy gave his friend a gentle fluffy hug, and then hugged Mr Voles too.

"The fluffiest friend in the world," murmured Mr Voles happily. "The fluffiest friend in the world."

# Scottish and Gaelic Words and Names

**Ailsa** (Scottish girl's name) is taken from the name of a Scottish island.

**Algy** is not a Scottish name. Algy came from a land far away across the sea, and his name is simply a short form of Algernon. But many people have asked how to pronounce Algy's name, so it is included here. It should be pronounced with a soft g sound in the middle: Al-jee.

**asking for** is a typically Scottish expression, which in casual English would usually be "asking after", meaning asking how someone is, or how they are getting on.

**aye** simply means yes. It is pronounced like eye.

**blether, blethering** (verb and noun) To blether is to have a long chat, often with plenty of gossip.

**brae** (noun) the steep side of a hill. Pronounced bray.

**Brianag** (Gaelic girl's name) is the name of an ancient Celtic goddess, said to mean strength. Pronounced roughly Bree-uh-nak.

**burn** (noun) a stream, brook or small river.

**canna** is the Scottish version of cannot or can't.

**ceilidh** (Gaelic noun cèilidh) is a traditional Gaelic social event or gathering, usually with music, which may include singing, playing traditional instruments, storytelling, and dancing. Pronounced kay-lee.

**concerning** (adjective) is a Scottish version of worrying.

**crottle** (noun) lichen, an English spelling of the Gaelic word "crotal" meaning lichen.

**dinna, didna** the Scottish versions of don't, didn't.

**"I dinna ken"** (Scottish phrase) means "I don't know".

**Dùn Bàn** (Gaelic place name) the White Fort. Dùn is the Gaelic word for an ancient hill fort. Pronounced roughly doon baan, with the a long, as it would sound if you drawled the word father.

**Eachann** (Gaelic boy's name) is the equivalent of the English name Hector. Pronounced with the E as in every, followed by han. Roughly E-han, with a barely breathed c in the middle (see end note on pronunciation).

**eldritch** (adjective) unearthly, strange and otherworldly.

**Flòraidh** (Gaelic girl's name) is a form of the Latin name Flora, pronounced roughly Flor-rai-ee.

**gloaming** (noun) twilight, dusk.

**hoodie** (noun) is a hooded crow. In the British Isles, hoodies are only found in north and west Scotland and in Ireland. They have black wings and tails, and black "hoods" on their heads, but are otherwise light grey.

**ken** (verb) know.

**laird** (noun) a landowner. Laird is a word which is often misunderstood outside Scotland. It is not a title for the nobility, like Lord in English, but simply means the owner of an area of land or the master of a grand house. Only in that sense can it be translated as "lord". So "the laird of the sky" means the master of the sky.

**loch** (noun) a lake if inland, or a fjord in the case of a sea loch. Scotland has plenty of both, and the term "loch" is used for all of them.

**lochan** (noun) a very small lake or a large pond or pool.

**nae** is the Scottish version of no. Pronounced nay.

**"nae bother"** is a common Scottish phrase meaning "no problem" or "that's all right", "don't mention it".

**no'** (adverb) is a common Scottish version of "not".

**o'** (preposition) is a common Scottish version of "of".

**Roni** (girl's name) is a version of the Scottish girl's name Rhona (Rona in English). Pronounced R-oh-nee.

**Ruaridh** (Gaelic boy's name) means reddish-brown (ruddy). Pronounced roughly Roar-ree.

**skerry, skerries** (noun) A skerry is a small rocky island or a rocky reef.

**"That's you"** is a typical Scottish phrase, often used on its own. It does not translate well into English, but usually means something like "you're done", "that's been done for you", "that's your problem sorted out", "that's your business finished", and so on, depending on the context.

**wee** (adjective) small.

*A note on pronunciation*
The spoken Gaelic language has a very soft sound. The "ch" sound in English versions of Gaelic words, such as lochan, is therefore soft, and is not pronounced like the ck in clock, nor like the ch in church. Instead, the c is almost lost, just faintly whispered, and the h is sounded in a slightly breathy way. So "lochan" is pronounced in two syllables: lo as in lock, and han as in handle, with a barely breathed c in between.

When the consonants dh follow a vowel together, they are usually silent, so the dh is not sounded in ceilidh, Flòraidh or Ruaridh, for example.

# More Tales from the Adventures of Algy

An enchanting series of tales which transport you to the
beautiful wild west coast of the Scottish Highlands

## A Surprisingly Fluffy Bird
### Jenny Chapman

Algy is completely and utterly lost – at sea! When his
tiny raft emerges from the swirling mist, Algy finally sees
the rocky coast and hills of a foreign land, but can he
manage to reach the shore and survive in this strange new
place? The first book in the series, this thrilling story of
endurance and achievement tells of Algy's arrival on the
west coast of the Scottish Highlands: a tale of dangers
and misfortune overcome, funny friendly creatures and
mean nasty beasts, and a surprisingly fluffy bird… Algy!

## The Magical Midwinter Star
### Jenny Chapman

In the chilly gloom of his first northern winter, Algy
finds it hard to stay cheerful… until he discovers some
mysterious objects in the rock pools and hears about
a midwinter celebration which used to take place
long ago, by the light of a magical star. Determined
to bring light and joy back to the darkness, Algy
has to face the dangers of a harsh Highland winter,
but with the help of his delightful old friends and some
very funny new ones, the story reaches a magically happy
conclusion. A perfect winter bedtime story.